PETAL PLUCKER

Funny, charming, and utterly captivating! I devoured this sparkling read.

— ANNIKA MARTIN, NEW YORK TIMES
BESTSELLING AUTHOR

Petal Plucker was funny, entertaining, fresh and fan-yourself-worthy . . . Their enemies-to-lovers romance is both charming, tender and steamy, and you'll love both of these characters (and their families!) and their sigh-worthy happily ever after.

— MARY DUBÉ, CONTEMPORARILY EVER
AFTER

Morland has created a masterpiece of a romance . . . one of my favorite [books] of the year.

— CRISTIINA READS

Humorous, raunchy, and refreshing, Petal Plucker has rightfully earned its way, in my opinion, as one of the best romantic comedy [books] this year.

— CAROL, TIL THE LAST PAGE

My One and Only

This book was gripping, well written & the chemistry between the characters sizzled throughout this wonderful read.

— AMAZON REVIEW

All I Want Is You

Another heartfelt, steamy, terrific story. This is an author who really knows how to create a story that catches a reader's attention and characters that capture her heart.

— BOOKADDICT

TAKING A CHANCE ON LOVE

Thea and Anthony are in for a surprise when it comes to the language of the heart . . . I am in awe.

— HOPELESS ROMANTIC BLOG

Then Came You

This story really pulled all my heartstrings. This was truly a beautiful story and makes you believe there really is true love out there.

ALSO BY IRIS MORLAND

ROMANTIC COMEDIES

He Loves Me, He Loves Me Not

Petal Plucker

War of the roses

LOVE EVERLASTING

including

THE YOUNGERS

Then Came You

Taking a Chance on Love

All I Want Is You

My One and Only

THE THORNTONS

The Nearness of You

The Very Thought of You

If I Can't Have You

Dream a Little Dream of Me

PETAL PLUCKER

THE FLOWER SHOP SISTERS

IRIS MORLAND

Happy Reading!

♡ *Iris*

BLUE VIOLET PRESS LLC

For Kit, because you gave me the idea in the first place.

PETAL PLUCKER

CHAPTER ONE

The day Jacob West walked into my store after breaking my heart nine years ago, I had just gotten my hand stuck in a vase and was trying rather desperately to free myself from its glassy confines.

I don't make a habit of getting my hands stuck in things, vases or otherwise. But today had been a shit-show, starting with my dad being afraid I was going overboard on the lily bouquets, and then my first customer complaining that her cut flowers had died. After two weeks, mind you. And then I'd dropped my nice little flower clippers inside a vase. Just as I'd gotten my fingers around the handle of the clippers, I realized that my wrist was too wide to get out of the vase.

And that was how Jacob found me. Because of course that would be how he first saw me after nine years.

"Dani?" he said, stepping toward the register. "Is that you?"

My back was turned, and I hadn't yet laid eyes on him. I muttered, "Sorry, one second." But when I whipped my head around and saw *that face*, the hand that had the vase attached

1

to it dropped to the counter and made such a loud sound that we both jumped.

Jacob looked—the same. But not the same. He was older, obviously, and his blond hair had darkened to a deep gold. His eyes were the same bright blue, but he had a few fine lines at the corners of his eyes. It only made him seem more interesting. Stubble dotted his jaw where once he'd been smooth as a baby. I couldn't remember him ever sporting facial hair as a teenager. Since he was so blond, I'd assumed his beard would grow in patchy or red.

Not that I'd ever thought that deeply about Jacob's facial hair.

He seemed taller than when he'd been seventeen, and he was more filled out. He wasn't that skinny teenager anymore, although he'd always been muscular in a skinny-boy kind of way since he played so many sports. But now he looked like a man, whereas before, he'd just been a boy. A boy who'd stood me up for prom, who I'd watched drive off with his ex-girl-friend when he should've been at my house putting a corsage on my wrist.

After that betrayal, I'd dated a bunch of guys who'd turned out to be weirdos, shady motherfuckers, or guys who worked for the mob but had neglected to tell me. Pretty hard to believe that I had trust issues, right? It *might* be the reason that I was twenty-six and had yet to have sex. I'd pretty much resigned myself to dying a virgin. Very tragic, I know.

It was amazing, though, how a history of lies and betrayal and ruined proms could fly out the window so quickly when face-to-face with someone. That someone being insanely, ridiculously, I-hate-my-fucking-life hot.

Why did he have to get *hot*?

I heard the dangerous saxophone sounds of "Careless Whisper" playing in my mind. I hadn't heard that song in my brain in nine years, and I hadn't missed it one bit. When I was kid, that song played like an absurd soundtrack every time I so much as saw Jacob's name written on top of his homework.

In seemingly slow motion, I watched Jacob approach the counter. Was this a dream? I pinched my leg with my free hand, but Jacob didn't disappear.

"Um, do you need help?" He pointed to the vase.

I'd forgotten about the vase. Nothing had mattered except that Jacob West was in the same place as I was. I picked up my hand, stared at the vase as if I'd just become aware of my current predicament, and said bluntly, "No."

"Are you sure?"

Like I was going to let Jacob help me. I said something vague and hurried to the back, desperately trying to get this thing off my hand. But to my immense humiliation, it wasn't going to budge. My wrist ached. I pressed my forehead against the cool wall and took in deep breaths.

Jacob. West. Was. Here.

Why was he here? He'd left Seattle right after high school and had been apparently making plenty of money as some kind of stockbroker in New York City. The last I'd heard, he had some penthouse and a hot girlfriend with fake boobs. I had a feeling that when you made enough money in a place like New York, the hot blonde with fake boobs came with the penthouse.

Okay, that was probably unfair. I'm sure his girlfriend had perfectly nice boobs, real or otherwise.

He was probably visiting his parents, but there was no reason he needed to come into my family's flower shop, Buds and Blossoms. He could go to *his* parents' flower shop if he needed to buy a bouquet for his girlfriend.

Yes, both of our parents ran flower shops, although I'd taken over my family's a few years ago. It's a long story full of rivalries and bitter mistrust. Think of our families like a version of *Romeo and Juliet*, except with the Montagues and the Capulets being obsessed with making bouquets.

I inhaled a few more deep breaths, willing my heart to slow. I let myself inhale the scents of flowers of all kinds, which normally I found soothing. But today, seeing the arrangement I was working on for the biggest design competition in the country made me want to throw up. Or maybe I just really wanted to throw the arrangement at Jacob's head.

Except I was extremely proud of this design: a purple monochromatic arrangement of roses, buckeye flowers and porcelain vines. I liked using flowers and plants that other people thought were common or weeds. It might have to do with the fact that I was named Dandelion, after that infamous weed.

But there were more important things at hand. I briefly considered simply shattering the vase stuck on my hand, but I didn't want to end up with glass in a rather important artery. Sparing myself the humiliation of asking for Jacob's help only to die from a dumb accident would be slightly worse than asking him for help. By a minuscule amount.

"Dani? Do you need help?" Jacob had followed me to the back.

Why did he have to be nice, too? I wished he would go away, except now I needed his help. He came to the doorway, and I could see him assessing what probably looked like a complete mess back here. There was a reason why it was called *the back*: it was so customers didn't get to see the not-so-pretty aspects of this job.

I thrust my hand at him. "Help, please."

His lips twitched, and my traitorous, stupid heart flip-flopped in my chest, just like it used to when we'd been kids. Why couldn't he have gotten fat and bald? Where was the justice in this world, I ask you? Boys who stand girls up for prom should end up with a beer gut, a large hairy mole on their face, and a distinct body odor that no deodorant could eradicate. It was only fair.

"How did you manage to do this?" Jacob peered at my hand. "I'm kind of impressed."

I rolled my eyes. "Save your compliments for later. My hand is starting to ache."

He took hold of the bulb of the vase, twisting it back and forth before he pulled so hard I was sure my shoulder was going to be pulled from its socket. Then with a pop, I was free, my clippers clattering to the floor.

I rubbed my wrist. "Thanks for that." I took the vase from his grip and got my clippers before asking, "What are you doing here?"

"Saving you from vases, apparently."

"No, I mean—why are you *here?* And don't tell me it's because you need a bouquet, because we both know that's not true."

"How do you know what I do and don't need?"

Good point. I shrugged, mostly because my heart was still pounding so hard that I was a little breathless. I wished rather belatedly that I had put on some mascara this morning, but today I was my usual, frizzy-haired self sans makeup.

Normally I didn't care, but I tended to care about a lot of dumb things when it came to Jacob West.

He's just some guy who you don't even know anymore. Don't get all weird.

We returned to the front finally. Jacob perused the flower arrangements that were for sale. "Do you run this place now?"

"Yes. I took over a few years ago when my dad retired."

"That's nice," he said, like we were catching up over lunch.

"You never did answer my question. Why are you here?"

Jacob leaned on my counter, all casual-like. He was way too good at casually leaning. "Can't a guy stop by to see one of his childhood friends?"

I raised an eyebrow. "A friend you haven't talked to in almost a decade?"

He winced a little. Damn, I was being a total bitch. Forcing myself to retract my metaphorical claws, I added, "Sorry. It's nice to see you. How's it been with you?"

"I'm actually back in Seattle for good."

I almost dropped the clippers again. "Why?" My voice was embarrassingly shrill at this point.

"My dad had a stroke recently, and he needs me to help take over the business."

I swallowed, a lump in my throat. My hands were shaking. Jacob West was back? Jacob West was going to be my direct competitor? Things were getting more complicated at a speed faster than light.

"I'm sorry to hear that," I managed. "About your dad, I mean. Are you living in the neighborhood?"

"I am. I just got a place a few blocks from my parents' place."

Oh God, that meant he'd be in *my* neighborhood. I lived in an apartment right next door to Buds and Blossoms, which also happened to be four blocks from both my parents' and Jacob's parents' houses. The thought of running into Jacob all the time made me want to crawl into a hole and die.

"Well, welcome back," I finally managed to croak.

His smile did annoying things to my insides. Oh God, was I going to do something stupid like get a crush on Jacob West *again?* I considered myself a smart woman. I knew how the world worked, even if my dating experience was limited to nonexistent.

Okay, yes, I was a virgin at twenty-six. What could I say? I'd been busy going to college, then learning the business, and then running it. I didn't have time for Tinder, hands down my pants, and a quick dry hump that ended with the guy collapsed beside me, snoring. I liked to tell myself I just hadn't gotten around to it, like someone else hadn't gotten around to cleaning out their garage. It'd happen—eventually. I wasn't in any hurry.

Suddenly, though, that whole virginity thing felt a bit bigger in my brain than cleaning out the garage. Because here I was, a virgin florist with a neurotic cat, and it just so happened that my first ever crush looked like some golden angel who was now wandering around my store.

Thankfully, Jacob wandering gave me a second to collect my thoughts. And to ogle him, if I were being honest. He wore what looked like an expensive leather jacket and a watch that gleamed in the natural light that flooded through the windows of the store. I wondered why his parents hadn't sold their business instead of having Jacob give up his career. I didn't know the Wests well anymore, but from everything I'd heard, they were immensely proud of Jacob's success.

Since I'd taken over running Buds and Blossoms, I was primarily in charge of designing arrangements and making bouquets. Currently we employed two other workers, Judith and Will. My dad still tried to help, but my mom would force him to come home, insisting that retirement meant *not working*. But he wasn't thirty years old anymore, and working sixty hours a week simply wasn't possible for him now.

Right now, the shop was filled with gardenias I grew in my apartment, along with the usual types of flowers people could easily recognize: roses, lilies, hydrangeas, tulips, daisies, to name a few.

All I wanted was to expand Buds and Blossoms and start giving classes while winning the most prestigious floral design competition in the country this summer. With the prize money and the year-long contract with a major wedding vendor, I could achieve all of my dreams with the added revenue. I didn't have time for complications.

Jacob West was a major complication.

Jacob bent down, and I couldn't help but ogle his ass. I wanted to touch it. Squeeze it. Make him groan. My lady bits perked up at the thought, but I had to douse them in cold water. Metaphorically speaking. Because no matter how amazing Jacob's ass was, it was not mine to grope.

He pointed to a gardenia arrangement. "This is nice. Did you make this?"

"I did the arrangement, yes, and I grew the gardenias." I couldn't keep the pride from my voice.

"I could never get gardenias to do what I wanted. Or maybe I just never had the patience for them." He touched one of the bright green leaves. "But my mom loves them. She has one that sits in our kitchen window."

"You just can't let them get waterlogged. They're fussy, but worth it."

"I know. Also, that sounds like every woman I've met." His fingers caressed a petal, and Christ, I wanted him to caress my petals in that very moment.

"Now you're just being sexist," I groused.

He flashed me a grin. "And you're just as charmingly sweet as when we were kids."

It was strange, having him reference the past so easily. Did he ever wonder what would've happened if we'd remained friends? *I doubt he's thought much about me in nine years,* I reminded myself.

"I was the kid who ripped up dandelions for fun. You knew what you were getting into," I said.

"Did I?" He sounded almost like he didn't know the answer himself. He gazed down at me, the laughter in his eyes suddenly gone. The moment felt almost unbearably intimate. But why should it? Jacob was nothing to me. He'd only been a mixture of nostalgic childhood memories and painful adolescent realizations until this random reunion.

"Why did you rip up dandelions?" he asked suddenly. "I don't think you ever told me why."

"Because I was a weird kid who also carried around plants in her backpack?"

"I'd forgotten that. I kept hearing rumors in high school that you were growing pot in your locker."

I scoffed. "You can't grow marijuana in a dark locker. At least, it would be a huge pain in the ass. It prefers a nice, humid climate."

"I'm so relieved you know the ins and outs of marijuana cultivation."

I bit back a smile. "Well, it's legal here now, so for all you know, I have a huge greenhouse overflowing with pot, with all kinds of species and strains."

He smiled, shaking his head. "You never answered my question."

Leave it to Jacob to pull me back to what he really wanted to know. Why had I ripped up dandelions? Probably because we shared a name, and for whatever reason, I had wanted to claim them. As I'd gotten older, I'd grudgingly begun to respect dandelions' hardiness. When you ripped them out of the ground, their root systems were so complex that they would grow back, like they hadn't even noticed that you'd tried to kill them.

"Well, since you answered mine. I guess I just liked to see if I could kill them," I said. Right then, the front door bell chimed, and a customer walked inside.

Thank God. This entire conversation was just getting weird.

"That's morbid." Jacob shook his head. "I'll take this one," he added, before he set one of the gardenia arrangements on the counter.

"I thought you said gardenias were too fussy for you?"

"Just because I couldn't get a flower to do what I wanted when I was younger doesn't mean I can't manage it now." His words held a promise that made me shiver, a flame curling inside me. If I weren't sane and aware of who I was, I would've thought he was flirting with me.

After paying, Jacob held his gardenia plant like a newborn

baby and saluted me. "See you, Dani. Don't get any more vases stuck on your hand."

"What did that young man say?" said my customer, who was the old woman who'd been angry that her cut flowers had died and who also tended to yell because she refused to wear her hearing aids. "You got mace stuck on your sand?" she yelled.

"Yes!" I yelled back, because that sentence made about as much sense as this entire day had—absolutely none at all.

CHAPTER TWO

I usually had dinner with my family every Sunday evening. My older sister, Marigold (who we all called Mari), sometimes joined us if she wasn't busy doing something with her fiancé, David. My younger sister, Kate, only joined us because the food was infinitely better than the stuff they served at the dorm cafeteria at UW, and, as she would elegantly put it, "I can't eat Chipotle every day or my asshole will explode."

It was three days after Jacob had visited Buds and Blossoms. I'd told no one of his moving back to Seattle, although I knew my parents wouldn't be thrilled. Actually, they *hated* him for what he'd done to me at prom. My mom had even cursed him using her most powerful crystals; my dad had gone so far as to call him a "selfish little shit." My dad never swore, so that was saying something.

So, I had no reason to tell them. Besides, it felt like a secret I'd rather keep for myself—a secret I could hold close to my heart and ponder over in the wee hours of the morning when I couldn't sleep. I still didn't know why he'd stopped by in the first place. My more negative side wondered if he had wanted to scope out Buds and Blossoms, but why now? They'd been our direct competitor for years. If they were just starting to snoop around, they were about twenty-five years too late. Then again, things were different now that Jacob was back.

"Dandelion, I'm so glad you're here," said my mom as she hugged me, as if I hadn't just seen her last Sunday. "Come help me pot these begonias. Your sisters are useless with plants."

"Mari is good with plants," I pointed out.

"She is, but she says she just got her nails done and can't handle the soil." My mom sighed, as if Mari had told her she was disowning the family entirely.

I went outside with my mom after saying hello to my dad. He was the one cooking dinner; my mom had a green thumb but zero cooking skills. One time she made us pancakes and had forgotten the flour. She'd basically made us curdled, milky eggs that had scarred us all for life. To this day, I couldn't eat real pancakes.

"I heard some interesting news," my mom said after we'd put on gardening gloves. "I heard that boy is back."

I didn't need to ask her who she meant. "And?"

She shot me a surprised look. "He broke your heart and that's all you have to say?" She clucked her tongue before picking up a begonia plant. "Move the dirt for me, will you? Apparently, he's back for good. Josie told me about it. His father had a stroke and wants him to take over the business." She snorted. "Like a boy like him could run a store like that. He'll run it into the ground, mark my words."

"Didn't he get an MBA?"

13

"So? It's one thing to know about the business side of things. It's another to understand the floral side of things. I bet that boy hasn't grown a plant since he left home." My mom said the words like you would say that someone hadn't bathed in ten years—with complete and utter disgust. The statement was immensely ironic, given that Mom had handled the business side of things for Buds and Blossoms since its opening.

I had no reason to defend Jacob West, yet I found myself doing just that. He had fucked me over quite thoroughly nine years ago. I had a right to be angry, but at the same time, my parents had never liked the Wests to begin with. When Jacob had stood me up for prom, they'd almost been strangely pleased, as if the universe had finally shown me the light. *What can you expect? He's a West*, they'd said over and over again.

"He stopped by the store," I said.

My mom froze. "What? Why?" She wiped her forehead, which left a streak of dirt there. "He must be trying to learn our secrets. Did he buy anything?"

"Mom, come on. He just wanted to say hello."

"I can't believe you're being this naive, Dani! That boy is no good." She wagged her finger in my face. "No good, you hear me? He wants to take over our store, maybe buy us out." She took another begonia out of its plastic container so roughly I stared at her in shock. My mom *never* handled plants with anything except gentleness. She usually treated them like delicate china dolls. She wouldn't even step on the dandelions in our yard, reasoning that they had a right to live as much as any other plant or animal.

"Mom, it's fine. He isn't going to keep coming around."

"Who isn't going to keep coming around?" Mari came outside, leaning against the doorframe.

With her long, auburn hair, milky skin and bright green eyes, Mari looked like something out of a magazine. She'd always been pretty, but when she'd started learning how to become a makeup artist in high school, she'd managed to turn herself into knockout. Everything about her was perfectly manicured, from her nails to her hair to her clothes. I don't think I've ever seen her with so much as a zit. A large diamond sparkled on her left hand. Her fiancé had proposed two months ago, and she'd been on cloud nine ever since.

I'd always thought her name was too banal for her. Marigolds were cute, but Mari herself was more like a hibiscus: eye-catching and gorgeous, her hair the deep red of the center of a hibiscus. I'd once told her that I'd thought of her compared to that flower, and she'd told me I was silly before going out and buying a hibiscus plant for her apartment.

I'd yet to understand what Mari saw in her fiancé, David. He was average in every way: average height, average appearance, average bank account. He talked of average subjects (the weather was his number one favorite), drove a Prius, and had a dog very aptly named Spot. He had no imagination; he thought gardening was pointless. He talked to me about the pros and cons of a traditional and Roth IRA for an entire evening once, and I almost died of boredom.

Mari was too vibrant for a guy like David, but she seemed happy. So when she told us she was engaged, we all acted like we were excited and gushed over her ring. At least he'd gotten her a nice, big diamond.

As far as Kate, she was more like me, in that she preferred sweatshirts to dresses and didn't know how to put on eyeliner. The only reason Kate didn't have a flower name like me and Mari was because my mom had been so doped-up on pain meds after Kate's birth that my dad had been able to fill in the birth certificate with a normal name. My mom hadn't been particularly pleased when my dad had told her what he'd done.

Kate was seven years younger than me and had been an oops baby. It had been strange, suddenly becoming the middle child after years of being the youngest, but Kate was such a mixture of enthusiasm and unintentional deadpan humor that it was difficult not to like her. Even if she'd liked to pluck blossoms from the flowers I had blooming in my window when she'd been little. In a twist of irony, Kate had grown up to have a completely black thumb. I'd been a little worried she was a serial killer when she was younger, but she'd only grown up to be a science nerd instead.

"No one is coming around," I said at the same time my mom replied, "That West boy. He's back."

Mari's eyebrows rose. "Realllllly?" she drawled. She crossed her arms. "I thought he lived in New York."

"Not anymore. And he came to Buds and Blossoms to scope it out." My mom took off her gardening gloves as she shook her head. "Dani was just telling me about it."

Hurt curled inside me—stupidly so—that my mom hadn't even considered that Jacob had come by to see *me*. But why would she? The only thing she knew was that Jacob had played a cruel prank on me nine years ago.

"Who's living in New York?" This came from my dad, and

soon Kate was standing on the porch, the entire family together.

I groaned inwardly. I didn't need Kate teasing me about Jacob, and I didn't need my dad warning me away from him.

"Jacob West is back. He's moved back to Seattle to take over Flowers. His dad had a stroke, in case you didn't know. He stopped by the store a few days ago to say hello. Nothing else happened and nothing else will." I stood up and went inside the house to forestall further questions. I heard Kate say, "What's her deal?"

Dinner was a little awkward after that. My mom kept shooting me concerned looks, while my dad kept asking me questions about how the store was doing. "Did you sell those peonies? They weren't growing well last time I checked" and "What are you planning to enter into the next competition? You can't keep doing these weird arrangements. You'll get pigeonholed. You don't want to be known as a designer who can only do one kind of arrangement."

Mari leaned over to whisper in my ear, "I want to hear all about Jacob." She was the only one who had an inkling of my prior feelings for Jacob. Even then, she'd never known the extent of it. It had been too humiliating to confess that I loved a boy who hadn't really cared about me, while Mari had to fend off boyfriends left and right. But I wasn't seventeen anymore. I wasn't going to wallow because, God forbid, some guy only saw me as a long-lost childhood friend and nothing else.

After dinner, my dad called me into his office, which was more of an indoor garden center. There a desk some-where amongst the plants, but it had been hidden long ago. His beloved orchids sat next to the large window that faced south, receiving lots of sunlight when Seattle felt like being sunny.

I touched a set of tiny seedlings on a chest of drawers. "Brussels sprouts?" I guessed.

My dad raised an eyebrow. "How could you tell?"

"Mostly because you always start your sprout seedlings this time of year," I said, smiling.

He chuckled. "Of course. Your old man is nothing if not predictable." He sat down in his favorite chair and began to prune one of his bonsai trees. He'd recently bought a few and had declared that he loved them almost as much as his orchids. "Sit down. I wanted to talk to you."

On the bookshelf across from where we sat stood dozens of trophies and ribbons: some were mine, while most were my dad's. Trophies I'd earned from floral designer competitions as a kid and teenager still resided here, while the ones I'd earned as an adult were at my house. I wasn't close to overtaking my dad's number, but I would by the time I was fifty if I kept winning at my current rate, I'd calculated.

"You remember this one?" My dad stood up and took down a trophy that wasn't remotely trophy-shaped, but instead a glass lily. "I was sure that girl who'd made the arrangement in the pumpkin would win, but you sneaked by her. You won by ten points." Pride lit his voice. "The one you did was pure genius."

"Oh, I remember," I said dryly. "You cornered the previous grand champion, and when she wouldn't tell you her soil composition for her orchids, she almost started crying. I remember, distinctly, security tried very hard to throw you out, but you bribed them with free bouquets for their girlfriends on Valentine's Day."

"A man has to do what a man has to do." My dad folded his hands. "Speaking of competitions, you haven't told me what you have planned for the LA show."

As a kid, I'd loved having these sessions with my dad to discuss my ideas for a competition. I traveled cities across the country, entering my arrangements for prizes and trophies, and every time I won, I loved making my dad proud the most. But every time I lost or didn't get first place, I always felt the failure immensely. My dad would look disappointed, give my shoulder a squeeze, and say, "Next time, kiddo."

Now, though, I didn't want to talk about my ideas, because my dad rarely understood them. Our design aesthetics were day and night: he thought I was too outlandish, that I missed the point entirely of what an arrangement was supposed to be. I always countered that his designs were too safe. He would then point out that he'd won more trophies than me.

He always pointed out that little fact, never mind that he was twice my age. He never took that tidbit into account.

"I haven't completely decided yet," I hedged. It was true—mostly. I was ninety-five percent sure at this point what I was going to do.

"What about an arrangement with peonies and dusty miller? It could've used more greenery and it rightly won fourth place, but I thought you could improve upon the design." He pulled up a photo on his phone, only to show me one of him lying on a bed, buck naked. The only good thing was that he had his hand covering his junk.

I let out a screech of horror. "Oh my God, Dad! What the hell?" I covered my eyes and shook my head, as if I could dislodge the photo from my mind. Fuck, I'd see my dad in that pose until I was dead, wouldn't I? I'd probably go to hell with that memory in my mind.

He glanced at his phone. "Oh. Yes. Oh dear. Your mother and I—"

"Do not finish that sentence. Don't even think it."

He cleared his throat, a faint blush tingeing his cheeks. "*Anyway.* Here's the photo."

I was afraid to look now. What if he accidentally swiped to a dick pic? I'd never recover. I really would die a virgin.

I looked at the photo—thankfully, it was just an arrangement—and said, "That's nice."

"I agree. You can make a better version of it."

I blew out a breath. "I don't want to do one with dusty miller. It's safe. Boring. They always look like wedding flowers."

"Then what are you going to use instead?"

"I've already put together one with roses and buckeye."

My dad grimaced and rubbed his temples. "Dani, I know you're in some kind of phase right now—"

"Dad, I'm not thirteen."

"—where you think using flowers that aren't suited for arrangements is somehow more interesting, but we both know it isn't. Didn't you get second place last year when you did that one with ragweed?"

I gritted my teeth. "Yeah, but the judges were total hacks."

"I won't disagree." His lips tilted into a smile. "Look, sweetheart. You know I just want you to do your best. Take your old man's advice for once, huh? Thinking outside the box is all well and good, until the box turns into a spaceship and you're catapulting to the moon."

"That metaphor doesn't even make sense."

He patted my hand. "It does if you squint." He returned to pruning his bonsai tree, effectively dismissing me.

I kissed his cheek and headed home after saying goodbye to my sisters and mom. I'd tell Mari about the Jacob thing some other time; I didn't have the energy right now.

As I walked home, the summer sun just beginning to set, I felt a heaviness settle onto my shoulders. Not just because I'd gotten an eyeful of my dad—I shuddered at the memory—but because I wasn't sure I'd ever measure up to what my dad wanted me to be. He'd always pushed me to be the best, the smartest, the most ambitious. He'd always told me that my sisters were lovely girls, but I had grit. Gumption. And a thumb as green as his.

I also just realized that my parents had a better sex life than me. How tragic was that? I had cobwebs practically growing from my vagina and here my dad was, sexting my mom. Did they send each other lewd plant-metaphor sexts? *I can't wait to stroke your stamen. I'm dying to pet your pistil.*

"I need psychiatric help," I muttered as I climbed the stairs to my apartment. When I opened my door, my cat came bounding toward me.

"Hey, Kevin." I picked him up and he started purring. With only three legs and one eye, Kevin wasn't exactly a looker, but I adored him anyway.

I thought of Jacob suddenly. Was he alone in his apartment right now? Or with his parents? Or maybe his girlfriend had moved to Seattle with him. My stomach curdled at the thought, which was so very, very stupid.

Strangely, I wanted to trust him. I wanted to believe that he'd just come by my store to say hello, but I had no reason to trust him. Not really. He was my direct competitor, for one thing. Was he just another Scott or Paul, destined to show his true colors and disappoint me?

It's not like you're going to be dating him, my mind reminded me. *So there's no reason to get worked up over him.*

Jacob West had never been mine and he never would be. I needed to get off the damn spaceship my dad had talked about and get back to Earth before I got hurt.

CHAPTER THREE

I f you're thinking my lack of dating experience is because I've been pining for Jacob for nine years, then you'd be wrong.

I had enough self-respect not to keep pining for a guy who'd stood me up for prom. I might have pined for the *idea* of him, if you want to get existential about it. But did I cry into my pillow every night, wishing Jacob would show up at my dumpy apartment at UW and tell me he loved me?

Hell no. The only thing I was crying about in college was the fact that my biology professor refused to grade our midterms on the curve.

But my dating experiences were always a mess, no matter who I dated. My first boyfriend, Todd, was in my biology class in college, and he wore glasses that had such thick lenses that when he looked at you, he was bug-eyed. It was hard to take Todd seriously when he looked like he had magnifying glasses stuck to his face. But when he asked me out for coffee, I said yes.

Todd proceeded to tell me all about his collection of *Star*

Wars memorabilia, which would've been fine, if he hadn't insinuated that he'd really like me to dress up as Princess Leia. And not in her standard white dress, but in that ridiculous metal bikini. I didn't even finish my latte before I booked it out of there.

I went on a few dates with some other guys—Scott first, then Paul. Scott told me he worked in tech. He had a stable job, good family. He even owned his own home. Until I found out his name was not Scott, the only thing he owned was a tiny, hole-ridden houseboat on Lake Union, and that he really, really wanted me to join this great pyramid scheme with him.

Paul was the worst, though. I dated him for six months before I discovered that he was already married. With three children. We had been at our favorite Thai restaurant, and I'd just bitten into a spring roll, when a woman—who turned out to be his *wife*—stormed in, threw a glass of bubble tea into his face, and caused such a scene that the cops were called. Suffice to say Paul and I didn't last beyond that little nugget of information getting out.

My friend Anna kept telling me that I chose these guys for a reason. "You subconsciously knew they were creeps and that you'd never have to commit to them," she would always say. "How about you try dating someone you don't meet on Tinder?"

I tried my hardest to vet the guys I dated. I really did. As the years had passed, I developed what I called my Honesty Policy. I tried to be as honest as I could, and I expected the same of other people. Should've been simple, right? Except honesty is apparently one of the hardest things ever for people.

Quite coincidentally, I actually had a date with a guy I

hadn't met on Tinder, but on Bumble, the same evening Jacob had come into my shop. His name was Marcus, and he and I had been messaging via Bumble for a few days before he finally asked me out for drinks. He'd told me he was a computer programmer, that he thought it was cool I ran a flower shop, and he hadn't made any jokes about my full name being Dandelion. For me, that meant he was pretty much marriage material.

Marcus had chosen a brand-new bar in Belltown that was so dim I could hardly make out what he even looked like. He was tall, that I could tell. Dark hair, dark glasses. He was wearing either a blue or gray shirt. He pulled out my chair for me, so that was a plus.

"I always wanted to go to school for music, but my parents wouldn't pay for my tuition if I did. So now I'm a computer programmer," he said.

His voice was so bland that I couldn't tell if he resented his parents, was grateful to them, or was simply apathetic. "Do you ever want to go back and get a degree in music?"

"Why would I? There's no money in the arts."

"Well, sometimes it's not only about money."

He snorted. "Only a woman would say that."

The evening continued on in a similar fashion: he mansplained to me how to grow hydrangeas; he told me that he hadn't initially wanted to message me back but that he'd been feeling lonely so he decided, what the hell?

I found myself thinking about Jacob as Marcus talked. I realized early in the evening that he wasn't the kind of person to ask questions of other people, so I only needed to nod or say *hmm* a few times.

I couldn't imagine Jacob treating a date like this. But then again, what had I to base that assumption on? I didn't know him. He was still as charming as ever, still handsome and confident, but that didn't mean he'd want to listen to his date talk about her job or her cat or her parents. Yet despite my best efforts, I kept going over our meeting, wondering if my mom was right in that he hadn't wanted to see me at all but had wanted to scope out the store.

Maybe he wanted to see both you and the store? I thought, which was the dumbest thing ever. That wouldn't exactly be a compliment.

After an hour, I couldn't take listening to Marcus any longer. I'd rather go home and watch *Chopped* with my cat at this point.

"It's getting late," I lied. "I'm going to head out."

Marcus paid for our drinks—at least he knew enough about dating to do that—and tried to kiss me as I got into my car. But he ended up kissing my jaw and then giving me those awkward first-date hugs where both parties were stiff and self-conscious. He told me he'd call me; I didn't feel like reminding him that I hadn't given him my number.

I'd forgotten all about Marcus by the time I arrived home. My brain was on two things: work tomorrow, and Jacob. Mostly Jacob, if I were being honest. I couldn't stop obsessing over his motives. It shouldn't matter; he wasn't my problem. I didn't even like him. I wasn't a lovesick teenager anymore who was going to start writing *Mrs. Dandelion West* all over my notebook, surrounded by hearts.

I was an adult now who also had no intention of giving up my last name, because, to quote Gretchen Wieners from *Mean Girls*, "that's just like the rules of feminism."

I fell asleep watching an episode of *Chopped* where the

contestants had to make a dessert out of an ostrich egg, bitter melon, salsa, and barley, which sounded terrible no matter what you ended up creating.

The night after I'd first seen Jacob, I dreamed about him, because my life was a walking cliché. It started out inauspiciously: Jacob coming into Buds and Blossoms and ordering a bouquet of poison ivy. Since this was a dream, my dream self shrugged and went to the back to get my basket of poison ivy —as you do.

"Dani," said Jacob, his voice like melted chocolate wrapped in velvet and served up in a perfect gift box straight from Saks Fifth Avenue. "I've missed you."

My dream self smiled seductively. "I know you did." (Dream self was way more confident than my actual self.)

"I couldn't stop thinking about you. Every day for the past nine years, I wanted you. You're so fucking gorgeous. I'm hard just looking at you."

The dream escalated rather quickly after that. Jacob pushed the poison ivy bouquet aside, the glass shattering on the floor, as he yanked me into his arms. I felt up his torso, which was now blessedly shirt-free thanks to the magic of dreams. He had dark blond chest hair that rubbed against my aching nipples (my shirt and bra had also disappeared, praise the lord).

Jacob lifted me onto the counter and ripped off my jeans and panties in one go, his blue eyes like the blue of a flame. When he kissed me, my entire body shuddered. Even though this was a dream, I could feel the scratch of his beard against my chin. I could taste him on my tongue, and I felt my pussy grow wet from that simple imaginary kiss. One of his hands cupped my breast, the other parting my thighs. I arched against him, begging for more.

He touched my aching clit with infinite slowness, and for some reason, he wouldn't speed up. Apparently, even in a dream, I couldn't get Jacob West to do what I wanted.

"I always wanted you," he said.

"Even when we were kids?"

"Yeah."

At this point, his cock burst through his jeans like something out of the *Hulk*, but my dream self took it in stride. His cock was *huge*. I gasped. "Oh no, it'll never fit," I said.

"It'll fit, baby. It was made just for your pussy."

He thrust inside me to the hilt. I could feel an orgasm building inside me as he pounded into my wet pussy. He felt so big that I was sure he was going to tear me apart. Somehow, he managed to keep rubbing my clit as he fucked me, and I felt that familiar tightening in my belly that signaled that I was close.

Something sharp dug into my side, breaking my concentration. I tried to brush it away, but then it started really hurting. I was about to tell Jacob to stop digging his claws into my ribs when I woke up and realized the only claws digging into my ribs were my cat's.

"Goddammit," I said with a groan, flipping over and making my cat, Kevin, jump off of me with an annoyed yowl. I pounded my fist against my pillow. "I was just getting to the good part!"

Of course, now I was horny and desperate, and with Jacob's face in my mind, I strummed my clit until I came so hard my vision went a little black. I was gasping and sweaty, and so turned on that after letting my body come down for a few minutes, I was able to rub out another orgasm.

Damn. I had never been very good at getting myself to come more than once during masturbation. Apparently, Jacob brought out the big guns in that regard.

As I got out of bed and made breakfast, I wondered if I needed to get laid in general. Jacob had just awakened something inside me that could get relief through other means, or through another man. Hell, I could message Marcus, if I were really that desperate.

Except I didn't want Marcus. Despite it being the worst idea ever in the history of forever, I wanted Jacob.

Too bad that was never going to happen.

CHAPTER FOUR

A lthough my family was hardly best friends with the West family, they did live in our neighborhood. After Jacob had told me about his dad's stroke, I felt guilty that my parents would never send them a bland casserole and a Get Well card. So I made a quiche that I hoped was seasoned well, bought a card, and walked to the Wests' house to drop it off.

But when no one answered the door, I realized I probably should've called ahead. Not that I had their phone number, but I could've found it somewhere. Not wanting to just leave it on their doorstep for the raccoons to munch on, I walked over to Flowers to drop it off there. Judith had opened the store this morning, and I didn't need to be there until the afternoon shift.

It wasn't exactly a surprise to see Jacob again, but my heart did that annoying little kick it always did when I thought about him. I spotted him off to the side, helping a customer. I felt awkward with my quiche and card. Did I look around like I was going to buy something? Or did I just stand here and wait?

Jacob had just reached for a vase of lilies when his gaze caught mine. The customer also happened to reach for something, and I watched in horror and amusement as the customer's arm accidentally hit the base of the vase and proceeded to spill its watery contents all over the both of them.

"Oh!" and "Shit!" were said from both customer and Jacob. Jacob set the vase down, only for it to begin to drip water down onto the shelf below. Seeing Jacob actually frazzled and, well, *human*, was a unique experience for me.

Since Jacob hadn't gotten to this point yet, I set down the quiche and grabbed some paper towels from underneath the counter. I was well-versed in floral-related accidents, that was for sure.

"I'm so sorry," Jacob kept saying at the same time the customer kept also apologizing. It was basically an apology battle. It looked like most of the water and bits of lilies had splashed onto Jacob; the customer had managed to get little more than some water on her shoes and the arm that had collided with the vase.

I cleaned up the water from the floor as best I could after I'd handed the two of them paper towels to dry off with. "Dani, you don't have to clean that up," said Jacob.

"Go get that wet apron off." I smiled wryly up at him. "I'll take care of the rest."

He looked grateful, hurrying to the back. I helped the customer and, since Flowers had an old register that didn't involve any codes to enter to use it, I was able to get her checked out by the time Jacob came back out.

"Did she leave?" he said.

"Don't worry, I took care of her."

I looked him up and down. His apron had kept his clothes dry, except for a few water spots here and there. Today he wore jeans and a green sweater. He looked delicious in green, and if I weren't careful, I'd start munching on him like the snack he was. *Nom nom nom*, my brain and libido went. *Nom nom nom, J is for Jacob and he is yummy in my tummy.*

"Thank you, then." He rubbed the back of his neck. "I guess we're even now."

I was confused for just a second before I laughed. "Oh, yeah. I guess we've both been attacked by vases now. It comes with the territory."

He pointed to the quiche, which was probably cold by now. "Did you bring me food?"

"It's not for you. I mean—it could be. It's for your parents. I felt bad after you'd told me about your dad. It's a quiche," I added, as if that detail were actually important.

Surprise crossed his face. He looked at me like he couldn't quite make me out. "Well, then I guess I should thank you a second time."

As the silence blossomed between us, I glanced around Flowers for the first time in years. Last time I'd been here I'd been in elementary school. It looked much the same, except for the new paint on the walls. I could've sworn they'd had more bouquets and arrangements on sale, but they might've moved toward custom orders. I had no idea. My dad had been the one to pay attention to those details.

"Besides getting all wet," I said, because, for some inexplicable reason, I didn't want to leave, "how's it going with the whole taking-over-the-business thing?"

"Well, I look like I fell into a rosebush," he said as he

showed me his scratched palms. "And I forgot to use flower food in the bouquets so now they aren't blooming as much as usual. But the customers are nice, so I'll figure it out. I always do."

He sounded so confident in his abilities that I felt irritated. I'd worked my ass off to get where I was. Did he really think he'd learn everything he needed to know by magic?

"I'm sure you will figure it out. You always seemed more than capable when we were younger. You were the most popular boy in school. You were the person everyone wanted to be: perfect in every way." I added in a harder voice, "You were prom king of our little universe."

He stilled at that last comment. "I'm not perfect." Now he sounded really annoyed.

"Maybe not, but close enough."

He gestured toward where the vase accident had happened. "Do things like that happen to perfect people?"

"That's not the point."

"What *is* the point? Enlighten me."

"You act like this is all going to be so easy. You'll just 'figure it out,' and it'll just magically come to you."

"Is it really that complicated to understand? Running one flower shop?" He cocked an eyebrow.

I was rather tempted to throw another vase of lilies at him. "You're so arrogant."

"Not arrogant. Just confident."

I scowled. "God, you're still as much of a butt-face as when we were kids."

Suddenly the mood lightened, and he laughed. "Seriously? 'Butt-face'?"

"Yeah. It seemed the most accurate descriptor I could think of."

"You use the word 'descriptor' but can't think of a better insult than 'butt-face.' " He shook his head. "I think you need to work on your shit talking."

"Are you going to tutor me in how to insult people now?"

"Are you suggesting that you'd like me to?" He stepped closer to me, until I could make out the light blue circle around his pupils. "Why do I feel like you'd make a terrible student?" he said softly.

I swallowed, my throat dry. "Pretty sure I got better grades than you."

"I'm not talking about letter grades. I'm talking about a willingness to bend. Are you flexible, Dani? Because right now, you're about as rigid as a board."

I also thought of that ridiculous sex dream I'd had, and I wondered a bit wildly if he somehow knew I'd been having wet dreams about him. Right then, I was hot and I was cold. I wanted to jump his bones and throw something at his head.

I was pretty sure he was flirting with me. That realization in and of itself was astonishing. He could get any woman he wanted and he was flirting with *me*? Maybe he'd hit his head recently and had yet to fully recover.

For a long time, I wondered if there was something wrong with me, because I'd never felt whatever it was that people called chemistry with a man. The ones I'd dated had always either bored me or left me cold. The few times I'd made out with them, my mind had wandered, or I'd been too focused on how wet everything was—and not in a good way, either.

But right now, I felt that thrum of sexual tension that had

been elusive for me for so long. I watched as Jacob's pupils dilated, and I knew he felt it, too.

"I'm not rigid," I said, sounding breathy. I *never* sounded like that around men. Soon I'd be batting my eyelashes if I weren't careful. "I just know what I want."

"Why do I feel like that's not true?"

"And why do I feel like I'm talking to the Cheshire Cat? Saying everything but nothing at all. Go hang out in your tree and terrorize other dumb girls, Jacob."

"But you're so good at insulting me that it's almost impressive."

He'd leaned closer toward me, and I could smell his cologne: it was spicy, woodsy. It made me think of falling into his bed and feeling the rough calluses of his fingers against my skin as he moved down my body.

I was out of sorts, off-balance, and it was because of this man. I'd convinced myself that I'd gotten him out of my system years ago, but here I was, once again getting very close to becoming a googly-eyed, lovesick idiot panting after him.

Where the hell was my self-respect? Apparently, it had disappeared the second Jacob had appeared.

I stepped away from him. I was better than this. Jacob was my direct competitor. It was our jobs to steal business from each other. Which meant that I couldn't trust him, no matter how much I wanted to.

Yet I still found myself looking around Flowers. It was partly out of curiosity, and also partly out of a desire to know my competitor. I had been here once as a kid, and it hadn't changed much since then. It was smaller than Buds and Blossoms, and it didn't have many arrangements you could come in and buy. I assumed that most of their revenue came from specially made arrangements and from things like wedding, funerals, proms—all the life events a person would need flowers for. Strangely, there weren't many plants in here at all, except for a dried-out fern on a shelf overlooking the front counter and a few vases of flowers, including the lilies that had been spilled.

"Did you really come here just to drop off a quiche?" Jacob's voice was wry.

I jumped, laughing a little. "Sorry. I haven't been here in so long. Curiosity killed the cat, you know."

The real eye-catcher in this place was a crescent-shaped arrangement of red roses that had been placed right next to the single window overlooking the street. I wondered who'd made it. Since Jacob's dad had had a stroke, I'd assumed he'd been too ill to continue designing, but maybe he'd recovered enough already. I didn't feel like I had the right to pry.

I didn't hear Jacob come up behind me until he said, "I think I know what you're doing."

I turned, and my breath caught when I saw how close he was to me. I could make out the dark blue around his pupils, whereas the outer rim of his irises was a paler gray-blue. He had absurdly long lashes, and as a woman who had tried her fair share of mascara, I found it rather irritating.

Despite the long lashes, pretty eyes, and working in a flower shop, he still managed to exude masculinity. Maybe it was the confidence that he wore so easily, or how any parts of him that were pretty were overshadowed by the strength in his arms, or the firmness of his jaw, or the width of his shoulders. I had a distinct feeling that *strong* and *firm* were two of the best adjectives to describe Jacob West.

"What am I doing?" I said.

"You're here to steal all of our secrets."

I snorted, only because my mom had said the same thing about Jacob. "What, like your secret ingredient? What's in the fertilizer, Jacob? Please tell me so I can make a fortune." I batted my eyelashes.

He bit back a smile. "You're different than when we were in high school," he mused.

"Um, I should hope so. If I was the exact same as when I'd been a teenager, I'd be concerned."

"No, I don't mean how you look, but that is different, too, though not by much. I recognized you immediately." He peered into my face, like he could find all of my secrets and hoard them for himself. To keep myself from squirming under his scrutiny, I stared at him, too, which made him full-on smile.

"Have you figured me out, yet?" I said.

"No, but I think I will."

To my surprise, he reached out and plucked something from my hair, but he didn't move his hand right away. I waited from him to step away, but his gaze moved from my eyes to my mouth. Electricity seemed to crackle between us. My mouth went dry as I wondered if he was going to kiss me, right here in the middle of his store.

The front door jingled. Jacob stepped back, holding up a bit of white. The moment collapsed like a house of cards.

"Petal," he said. "In your hair." He twirled the petal between his fingertips.

Heat made my skin prickle. My lips felt swollen, even though he hadn't so much as touched me there.

"Do either of you work here?" said the woman who'd just

come into the store. She was about two seconds from tapping her foot.

I stammered out a goodbye and hurried to Buds and Blossoms, wondering what the hell had just happened.

Had I imagined the entire thing, or had Jacob actually wanted to kiss me?

CHAPTER FIVE

By the age of seventeen, I had fallen in love with Jacob three times.

The first time I fell in love with Jacob, I was five. I'd just started kindergarten, and it was the first time I was away from home all day. I usually spent most of my time pulling up dandelions from the field next to the playground, my mission in life to find every dandelion in existence. It was a tough job, considering that dandelions were everywhere I looked.

But I had a legitimate reason for this obsession. My name was Dandelion, and each flower I found was an extension of myself. Except I didn't think of it in those terms at that age. I mostly just liked ripping the plants out of the ground and enjoyed the sound the roots made when they tore. I was a bloodthirsty little weirdo in those days.

Jacob joined our kindergarten later in the year when his family moved into our little Wallingford, Seattle neighborhood. Initially, my parents were happy to make vegan casseroles galore for the Wests—until my parents learned that

Jacob's parents were opening a flower shop of their own not even a mile from ours.

"They couldn't have opened one in Fremont?" my dad bellowed every night for a month. "There aren't any over there and God knows those hippy freaks love smoking all kinds of plants! Who does that, though? Isn't that illegal?"

"Honey, this is America. Capitalism is never illegal here," said my mom.

"Maybe they just wanted to start their own store," said Mari with a shrug, a bit too wise for her age.

In my mind, Jacob West and his parents were the enemy. I hadn't met him yet, but I knew he would probably be worse than our class's bully, Tommy Hedrick. He probably pushed girls into mud puddles and tried to pull down their shorts when they were on the jungle gym. He probably picked his nose and kept a collection of boogers under the lunch table until the teachers complained and some poor janitor had to scrape off the offending bits of snot.

The following Monday, I was prepared to ignore Jacob West and show him that his family was basically evil incarnate. Anything that threatened Buds and Blossoms was a threat to *me*. Maybe if I were mean enough to him, he'd cry and his parents would move somewhere else.

But when I met Jacob, I realized that he didn't look remotely like Tommy Hedrick. He had hair that was so blond it was white, and he was tall and lanky. He had freckles all over his face, his nose sunburned. He looked like any other boy I'd ever met, and I had met at least a dozen in my short life to know what boys were like.

I said hello. He said hello. And I assumed that would be our last interaction.

Jacob West did not go away. He found me on the playground and asked me questions about why I was yanking dandelions out of the grass. I told him it was because I wanted to. He took that answer in stride and sat down beside me. He began to pull up dandelions, too, until we'd amassed a pile of yellow flowers that looked like bits of sunshine had fallen from the sky.

Jacob didn't say much that day. He didn't say much the next day when he joined me again with my dandelion plucking. At first, I tried my hardest to get away from him, but either he didn't get the hint or he didn't care. Finally, by the end of the week, I'd accepted that he'd join me on the hill where there were tons of dandelions, no matter how many I pulled up.

"Do you like the yellow ones or the puffy ones?" asked Jacob as he blew a cotton-headed dandelion into the breeze.

"I don't like any of them."

He frowned. "Why?"

"Because."

I didn't know why, really. I just knew that I didn't like my name, and I didn't like the flower associated with it. Besides, there was something rather thrilling about pulling up all those plants and making a giant pile.

"I like them," said Jacob. He took a few of the yellow dandelions and began to weave them into a crown. "They're pretty."

I snorted. Clearly Jacob wasn't as smart as I thought. He probably *did* pick his nose like Tommy.

But when Jacob put the finished dandelion crown on my head, smiling his gap-toothed smile, a butterfly fluttered inside my stomach. I didn't know that was possible. I wondered if I'd swallowed one by accident. It was the only thing that would make sense in my five-year-old mind.

When I got home, I pulled out the dandelion crown Jacob had made me. The petals were already turning brown, but I found myself placing it gently inside a shoebox and hiding it under my bed. Sometimes when I couldn't sleep, I'd pull that shoebox out and gently touch the dried flowers, reminded of that fluttering butterfly in my stomach each time.

Jacob and I became tentative friends over the next few weeks. He would join me on the jungle gym with my best friend, Anna; other times he'd play tag with the other boys and ignore us girls entirely. As the days got colder and we didn't have recess outside as much, I didn't have as many opportunities to pull up dandelions with Jacob. I missed it. I missed him talking about his favorite Power Ranger or his new pug puppy, Renaldo.

But I never told him that. He was a West, and my parents had told me and Mari time and time again that we weren't to have anything to do with that family.

"Apparently they sell silk flowers in their store," my mom said with a shudder over dinner one night. "Right beside the real ones, as if no one would be able to tell the difference. Why don't they just open up a Michael's and start selling ugly Christmas decorations while they're at it?"

"I don't care what they sell. It's that they opened a store so close to ours without even talking to us about it first. It isn't neighborly." My dad stabbed his fork into his seitan meatball with gusto. "Good people don't do things like that. They just don't."

I swirled my edamame pasta on my fork and almost bit my tongue in half. I hated lying to my parents, but I also hated the thought that I wouldn't get to hang out with Jacob West ever again.

I was torn between two worlds, a Juliet pining for her Romeo as our Montague and Capulet parents dueled over floral arrangements.

It was close to Halloween when Jacob became something more to me than a friend. It was a warm day for late October, and since Anna was sick at home with a cold, I was mostly on my own at school. I decided to go pluck some dandelions from my favorite hill. I hadn't done that in over a month, and I'd barely talked to Jacob in as long. I hoped he'd notice what I was doing and would come over. Maybe he'd make me another flower crown. I'd tried making one on my own, but it hadn't come out like Jacob's. I wanted him to teach me how he did it.

I heard footsteps. Turning, I had a bright smile on my face, only to realize it wasn't Jacob: it was Tommy. And he had that stupid smirk on his face he always got when he was going to do something gross. I stood up and pointed at him. "Go away!"

Tommy kept coming closer and closer, and soon he was raising a giant earthworm wiggling in his thick-fingered grasp. I could almost hear the silent screams of the worm as it thrashed. Tommy grabbed me by the back of my shirt. I tried to make a break for it, but Tommy was basically the size of a third grader. I was doomed.

I thrashed like that earthworm. I saw my life flash before my eyes. I could feel the worm in my shirt and it would be muddy and cold and slimy and what if it bit me? Did worms have teeth? What if I died? I didn't want to die just because Tommy was the worst human in existence.

But a second later, I didn't feel the cold slide of the worm against my back. I heard Tommy grunt, and then I watched Jacob pounce on Tommy like some kind of skinny tomcat trying to fight a bulldog. Tommy tried his best to get Jacob off of him, but Jacob was tenacious.

"Run, Dani!" said Jacob.

But I wasn't going to run. I threw myself into the melee, tackling Tommy. It soon turned into a wrestling match between the three of us, and by the time one of our teachers broke up the fight, we were muddy and sweaty and bruised.

As for me, I felt exhilarated. I smiled at Jacob. He smiled that gap-toothed smile at me. He was my savior, my hero.

I fell in love with him right then and there. That was just the first time, though.

CHAPTER SIX

My entire apartment was soon covered in supplies, sketches, flowers, and greenery for the design I was doing for the competition in Los Angeles in two months. For the first few rounds of design, I used silk flowers to save some money, but it really wasn't the same as using actual flowers. Silk flowers didn't stand or bend the same way real ones did.

I considered following my dad's advice and creating a more traditional design. Using an array of pastel-colored roses, I created an arrangement that, although pretty, looked like it had come straight out of a wedding banquet hall. I ended up donating it to my next-door neighbor, my sisters, and even my mailman when my apartment became so full of various arrangements that I couldn't use my kitchen table to eat breakfast.

My favorite so far was the arrangement I'd done with roses, buckeye, and porcelain vines, but I wasn't convinced it was enough to win. So I'd started over, confused on how I should proceed.

I was also throwing myself into designing because I didn't

know what the hell to do about Jacob. He'd almost kissed me and then…nothing. Although he lived only three blocks from me, I had no idea exactly which building that could be. I wasn't desperate enough to go knocking on random doors, demanding to know where he was. An almost-kiss didn't mean anything would happen between us.

It was on a Thursday, a week after Jacob had almost kissed me, that I came home, bleary-eyed and exhausted, with a bouquet of lilies to use in my next arrangement. I never brought lilies home because they were deadly to cats, and Kevin wasn't going to win any awards for intelligence. But I really wanted to include lilies in this next attempt, so I figured I'd hide the lilies in a cabinet and work on the arrangement with Kevin locked up in my bedroom.

Sometime after midnight, I woke up to the sound of something digging around. I groaned, figuring that Kevin had decided to rip up a paper bag that I'd left on the counter. Not wanting to clean up a whole bunch of shredded bits of paper in the morning, I lurched into the kitchen, only to find that Kevin had gotten into the cabinet with the lilies.

I awoke instantly. Grabbing Kevin, I looked him over. He had yellow pollen on his whiskers. I wiped it off frantically, knowing that even a tiny bit of lily pollen could make a cat seriously ill. He seemed fine, but I couldn't take any chances. I practically threw him into his carrier, put on my flip-flops, and drove straight to the emergency vet.

"Please don't let my cat die," I kept saying, over and over again, as I drove the mile to the vet. Kevin yowled unhappily from the backseat, which was a good sign. But when he grew quiet after I'd parked, I was close to throwing up.

Before I knew it, I was in the lobby, waiting for the vet to check over Kevin. I realized that the shirt I'd thrown over my sleep cami was inside out, and that I'd put on two differently colored flip-flops. I'm sure my hair was a wild mess; I hadn't even put on a bra, I'd been in such a hurry. I considered calling Anna or Mari, simply to have someone to sit with me, but I was such a mixture of exhaustion and terror that I couldn't make a decision about who would be better to call.

The vet tech took me back to one of the exam rooms, but Kevin wasn't in there. I wanted to throw up. If my stupid mistake had killed my cat, I'd never forgive myself. He'd already managed to survive with only three legs and one eye. Surely something like a lily wouldn't kill him off.

"Hi, Dani," said the veterinarian. "This sure is a blast from the past, isn't it? When I heard someone named Dandelion had brought in our next patient, I knew it had to be you."

I started in surprise when I realized it was Tiffany McClain, who'd put a fake valentine on my locker in the eighth grade and who'd been Jacob's ex-girlfriend. The same ex-girlfriend he'd driven off with on the night of prom.

Despite the late hour, she looked perfectly put-together: her blonde hair curled, her lipstick a pinky nude that suited her complexion. I'd had a vague recollection that I'd heard somewhere that she'd become a veterinarian, but I'd had no idea she practiced nearby.

Of course the night I ran into the girl who'd made my life hell as a teenager would be when I had crazy hair, an inside-out shirt, and two differently colored shoes.

"We gave Kevin an examination, and he seems okay," she said, smiling reassuringly. "But we'll keep him for a few more hours to make sure."

I let out the breath I'd been holding, perilously near tears.

The thought of crying in front of Tiffany McClain was more than I could bear, though. Sure, she was nice *now*. But I still remembered that fake valentine she'd taped to my locker. More importantly, she'd been the reason Jacob had stood me up. I wasn't absolving Jacob of guilt—not by a long shot—but it was more that he'd chosen her over me. That still hurt, even if it had become a vague hurt as the years had passed.

"You were smart to bring him in so quickly," said Tiffany.

"I never bring lilies home, but today I wasn't thinking. I did hide them, though. Kevin is just...determined."

Tiffany chuckled. "Based on the fact that he doesn't have an eye or one of his legs, that would make sense." She wrote something down and then added, "I'll have the vet tech bring him in here so you can see him for yourself. You're welcome to stay or go home while we watch him. We'll call you if anything changes, of course."

A vet tech brought Kevin to me, a yowling ball of fur, and I hugged him so close his yowling almost broke my eardrums. I let out the tears I'd been holding, relief making me weak. "You stupid, stupid cat," I muttered into his fur. "I hate you. You almost gave me a heart attack tonight."

I considered going home, but I knew I wouldn't be able to sleep. I hung out in the waiting room, watching people bringing in their dogs and cats. One woman had a cat that'd gotten run over by a car, poor thing; another woman brought in her dog who'd eaten some old Valentine's Day chocolate. Right as the woman was telling the receptionist the story, the dog puked what I assumed was the chocolate all over the white tile.

I'd just dozed off in my chair when a hand touched my shoulder. "Dani?"

I lurched awake. Tiffany stood over me. How did she manage not to have circles under her eyes when it was 3:00 AM? It was impressive. I wanted to know what magic spell she used to achieve that.

"What's wrong?" I blurted.

"Nothing. I just thought you'd like this." She handed me a cup of tea. "You should be able to take Kevin home soon."

It was such a strangely kind gesture from the same girl who'd done her level best to humiliate me more than once that I was totally nonplussed. I took the tea and half-wondered if this were another prank. Then again, if it were, it wouldn't be a very good one since the only other person around was the receptionist, who was currently playing on her phone.

I'd always wondered if Tiffany had been aware of Jacob standing me up. Had she been in on it? All I'd known was that they'd gotten back together the day after prom.

Tiffany sat down next to me, her hands in her lap. "You might think this is weird," she said all of a sudden, "but I've been meaning to get in contact with you."

I sipped my tea, but at her words, I accidentally inhaled and ended up choking. Coughing, tears leaking from my eyes, I tried to tell her between wheezes that I was fine. God, could this night get any worse?

Once I'd stopped coughing and crying, she said, "I just wanted to apologize. I never did, you know."

"Apologize for what?" *For which thing, exactly?* I wanted to ask.

"I'm sure you don't remember, but it was in eighth grade. I wrote this stupid valentine and put it on your locker. It was mean. I'm sorry."

"Oh. Well. It's okay. It was a long time ago."

Tiffany was called away to attend a new patient, leaving me to think. She'd always been on my list of shitty people: liars, assholes, people who dressed their dogs in sweaters. Once someone made the list, they never came off of it. Mostly because they never tried to get off of it. In my experience, once someone screwed you over, they'd do it again.

Yet Tiffany McClain, of all people, had apologized to me. It made me wonder if my list was too harsh, if I didn't give people a chance to redeem themselves.

Most dangerously, though, I wondered if I could let myself actually trust Jacob.

CHAPTER SEVEN

I pushed my empty wineglass across the bar. "Pour me another," I said.

"You're drinking white wine, not a snifter of brandy." Anna poured me another glass and leaned on the counter. "You gonna tell me what happened or am I going to have to beat it out of you?"

"You're shorter than me, so good luck."

"Stature has nothing to do with it." Anna flexed her biceps, which were, admittedly, rather impressive. "Spill, Dani, or you don't get any more wine."

Anna worked as a bartender in a dive bar in Fremont, about a half mile from my apartment. The counters and chairs were always sticky, and the place didn't sell anything more expensive than cheap vodka from Costco. Anna had been working here for the last three years, and thanks to her pretty face and ability to sweet-talk men, she earned great tips and could afford her studio apartment by herself. It also helped that her landlord was one of five people in the city who'd yet to raise the rent to an astronomical rate.

I signed, burying my face in my arms. "Jacob West is back," I mumbled.

"Yeah, I didn't hear anything you just said. Use your words."

I looked straight at Anna and enunciated, "Jacob. West. Is. Back."

Anna stared at me for so long I started to blush, which was stupid, because it's not like I'd done anything stupid. Not yet, anyway. But Anna was also the one person who knew exactly how obsessed I'd been with Jacob back in the day.

"Are you serious?" said Anna. "Are you fucking serious?"

"Totes. Where's my wine?"

"You aren't getting any until you tell me how you know this, why you know this, and why you didn't tell me immediately."

"Hey, I'm a paying customer—"

"You are not. You come here for free booze." Anna pointed a finger at me. "Spill."

Normally, Anna and I told each other everything: no topic was off-limits. She told me about her dates with men who ended up having a daddy/daughter fetish or who wanted to dress up as furries during sex. As for me, I rarely had any interesting sex stories to tell, but I always told Anna about what was going on in my life. We were best friends, after all.

"He showed up at the store last week. I also saw him again when I tried to take his folks a quiche. It was strange and I'm still confused about it all. That was about it."

"Hey, can I get a refill?" said a guy a few bar stools down. "Or are you two too busy gossiping?"

"Shut up, Donny. We're talking here." Anna waved a dismissive hand. Donny was a regular and was always complaining about the service, although I was pretty sure he enjoyed it when Anna insulted him. Donny muttered into his drink but didn't ask for a refill again for the next twenty minutes. How Anna managed to keep this job for three years, I had no idea. She was a terrible bartender.

"Okay, back to important things. What does he look like? Did he get fat and sad because karma is a bitch?" Anna's eyes sparkled.

I groaned. "No, worse: he got hot. Really fucking hot!"

"Well, that's just rude. But at the same time, if you keep running into him like this, maybe it's a sign from the universe."

"That my life is a joke and existence is pointless?"

"No, you nihilist. That you should jump Jacob's hot dick finally! You know you want to."

"That is a truly terrible plan. You're assuming Jacob would want me to jump him." Then again, he had been flirting with me at his shop: I couldn't be so dense not to notice that. But flirting didn't mean he wanted to fuck me. Probably. Maybe. Men were confusing.

"Wait," said Anna, as she finally got Donny's refill when he started complaining again. "Wait, why did he come by your store? Did you ever find out the real reason?"

"He wanted to say hello."

Anna frowned, and I could tell she was thinking something she was afraid to share.

"To repeat what you said earlier: spill it," I said.

She sighed. "I'm just worried, is all. If he's taken over Flowers, he might be scoping out your store."

"That's what my mom said. But why now? When we've

been competitors for decades now? Besides, what could he have seen just by looking inside our store for a half hour?"

"That's a good point. It's not like he broke inside and stole the secret sauce." Anna's eyes sparkled. "But most importantly, what did Jacob say both times you saw him? I want every single detail."

I told her about how he'd come to Buds and Blossoms, how he'd bought one of my gardenia arrangements, and how he'd brought up our childhood friendship. But when I told her about our encounter at Flowers, her eyes kept getting bigger and bigger until I was afraid they'd fall out of her head.

"Dandelion, you big dingus, he was flirting with you! Holy shit. Jacob West, Dani. This is amazing!"

"Just because he was flirting with me," I said, "doesn't mean he wants anything more than that. I mean, look at me."

Anna's eyes flashed. She always got pissed with me when I pointed out that I was the epitome of a Plain Jane. To me, I was being practical about my looks, but Anna seemed to take it personally. But she didn't understand that when somebody looked like me, you couldn't expect men to want you like they did when you looked like Anna or like Mari.

Anna was basically a guy's wet dream walking ever since she'd turned eighteen: a rosebud mouth, big boobs, a tiny waist, and the ability to mix any drink you could think of. When we'd been kids, she'd been as shy as me, but she'd blossomed during college. She'd soon figured out how to talk to men, to flirt with them, to make them want everything about her. I didn't hate her for it: in fact, I admired her for it. It was just how things were, end of story.

"You are beautiful—no, listen to me." Anna poked me in the shoulder with a French-tipped nail. "You are. I know you don't see it because of whatever dumb reason you decide to tell yourself, but you're gorgeous and if any guy can't see that, they suck. And I'm not humoring you, either. I'm not surprised Jacob flirted with you because he actually finds you attractive and smart and funny."

"More like awkward as hell, but I love you anyway." I patted Anna's hand. "It's not going to happen."

"Why? Because maybe you might risk being vulnerable? You'd have to trust somebody?" She put her hands on her hips.

I did not need this Dr. Phil talk right now. Putting down a ten-dollar bill, I said, "I'm heading home. Keep the change."

"Love you, bitch-face. But I want you to get some Jacob dick!" She almost yelled the words, which made Donny guffaw. I blushed and flipped her off. Anna just blew me a kiss in reply.

I walked home without really seeing where I was going. I didn't need to—I knew this route by heart. Since it was summer, the sun had only set an hour ago, even though it was close to eleven o'clock, and the night was warm. It wasn't a long walk, but it would help get rid of this nervous energy coursing through me every time anyone so much as mentioned Jacob's name.

Why did he still have to affect me so much? It was as if the years had never even happened, as if he'd never stood me up at prom and he'd never left Seattle. It was as if my brain was convinced he *had* taken me to prom, had told me he wanted me to be his girlfriend, and we'd dated all through college.

I kicked at a pebble, the sound of it bouncing along the sidewalk rather satisfying. I kicked another one, then another, watching them tumble downhill.

Although the streets were well-lit, it was still dark enough now that I failed to notice someone turning the corner at the bottom of the hill. I kicked a rock right at the same time the stranger crossed my path. I heard the stranger swear in surprise, and I jumped out of the way and almost fell into a bush.

"Are you okay?" I asked, guilt assailing me. Now I was assaulting random strangers? I needed to get my ass in line or somebody was going to get killed because I was too focused on this dumb crush I had.

The stranger moved into the light, grimacing. "Why do I have a feeling you knew it was me?"

It was Jacob. Of course it was. He was destined to see every stupid thing I did. Suddenly, I didn't feel so badly that I'd kicked a rock into his shin.

"How would I have known it was you? It's dark. I didn't see you," I said shortly.

"That was a terrible apology."

Despite my best efforts, I laughed. "I'm sorry. Really. Are you okay?"

Jacob was rubbing his shin and then picked up the offending rock, which was about the size of a half-dollar. "Christ, I'm glad I wasn't wearing shorts. You're a menace."

I was rather sad that he wasn't wearing shorts, only because I knew he'd have legs worth ogling, bruised and bloodied or not.

"Can you walk? Should I call an Uber? Or take you to the hospital?" I offered, rolling my eyes at his insult. It was a rock, not a grenade.

Jacob snorted. "I'm fine. You won't need to carry me home."

"What are you doing here, anyway?"

"I was down at Gas Works Park. Now I'm going home. Because I live nearby. Just like you do."

It was such a reasonable answer that I felt momentarily flummoxed. We were probably walking the same direction, but did we walk together? Or should I cut through the neighborhood to avoid the conversation that would definitely be awkward? Then again, if his leg was hurting and he needed help...

"Did you know that you narrow your eyes when you're thinking way too hard?" said Jacob.

"What?" I widened my eyes. "I'm not thinking."

"I'm not sure that's something you should admit." His smile sent my hormones into overdrive. He looked tousled, probably from the wind that came off the lake down at Gas Works. I wanted to kiss the indentation right above his collarbone.

"Well, I'm going home. Sorry about kicking a rock into your leg."

I started walking. To my dismay, Jacob followed me and began to walk right next to me, like we were a couple. When I reached my apartment, I said, "Thanks for walking me home, especially after the whole rock incident."

Jacob crossed his arms over his chest. "I actually live three blocks that way." He pointed to where we had already walked past. "So, either you can tell me to go home, or you can make up for breaking my shin by inviting me inside." His smile was wide, reminding me of the Cheshire Cat again.

Because I was Alice—completely out of my depth—I said, "If you want."

"I do want."

I shivered a little, but I told myself he only wanted to come inside to—I didn't know. Meet my cat? Men like him didn't invite themselves into my apartment. Correction: men didn't come into my apartment ever. Why would they, when I never got past the first or second date with them?

I heard Anna's words in my mind. *He was flirting with you, you dingus.* That could be the only explanation. I was officially in Wonderland, where none of the rules I knew existed.

CHAPTER EIGHT

My hand was shaking when I unlocked my door. Would he try to kiss me? Sleep with me? I barely stopped myself from laughing hysterically. But beyond some flirting, he hadn't expressed any other kind of interest. Shouldn't he, I don't know, ask me on a date first?

"Home sweet home," I croaked, flipping on the kitchen light. Kevin ambled up to me, his tail high and proud, until he saw Jacob. Instantly, he flattened his ears and hissed before darting into my bedroom.

"Um, sorry. Kevin isn't so great with strangers," I explained.

"Your cat's name is Kevin? And was he missing a leg?"

"Yes, and yes. He also has only one eye." I laughed at Jacob's expression. "He had a tough life on the streets before he was rescued and I adopted him."

Jacob gave me an odd look, and I wondered if I'd said anything stupid. Feeling flustered, I blurted, "You want anything to drink?"

"I'm fine." Jacob went to my living room window, which

faced south toward downtown, the Space Needle visible to the west.

I stared at Jacob's back, once again wondering why he'd asked himself into my apartment. He wasn't exactly jumping my bones right this minute, and I couldn't believe he'd come up just to look at the skyline, considering he'd just been down at Gas Works.

I floundered for something to say, but the silence kept stretching on and on. I couldn't figure out why Jacob had asked to come up in the first place. Anna's voice inside my brain kept getting louder, telling me that he *liked* me and wanted to spend time with me and touch me and kiss me and—

A hiss echoed in the room as Kevin spotted Jacob and proceeded to climb up his cat tree to survey his domain. Black and white with white socks, Kevin looked like a guy who'd gotten dressed up in a tux but had been mugged outside a fancy gala. His one green eye narrowed as he stared Jacob down.

"Your cat is terrifying," said Jacob.

"He's all bark and no bite. I just never have anyone over so he's not used to strangers." I winced, realizing what exactly I was saying. But when I saw Jacob's gaze heat, suddenly that embarrassment turned to desire, pooling low in my belly.

I went over and stroked Kevin behind his ears because I needed to do something. He started purring, adding in a few growls to remind Jacob that he still wasn't welcome. But my attention was solely on Jacob: the way he cocked his head to the side as he watched me. The way strands of his hair fell across his forehead. He suddenly reminded me so much of the boy I'd once loved that my chest hurt. Memories—both good and bad—tangled together in this present moment.

"Do you miss New York?" I asked, because it was the only thing I could think of.

"Sometimes, but every day that passes, I don't think about it as much. I know everyone harps on the Seattle Freeze, but New Yorkers are basically made of ice compared to people here."

"I'm sure Seattleites are as nice as Canadians in comparison."

His lips tilted up in a smile. "Basically."

"But your job? Do you miss it? This whole taking over your parents' business has to be a huge change," I pressed.

"It is. But I wanted to do it."

"Really? And you wanted to give it all up?"

"It wasn't so much I wanted to if other things hadn't pushed me to make that choice. But I needed to come back, I guess would be more accurate. I needed to come back and take care of my parents."

I had a hard time believing it. He'd been a successful stockbroker and living in one of the most exciting cities on earth. He'd gotten out of his parents' flower bubble, whereas I was still living in mine. It was a comfortable bubble, I had to admit, but sometimes I wondered if I'd sold myself short by going to school here and never leaving.

"Sometimes people expect things of you," he said, almost to himself, "but you can't live up to those expectations. It just isn't going to happen."

"I have a hard time believing you couldn't do anything you set out to achieve."

A muscle ticked in his jaw. Once again, I was reminded

that I didn't really *know* this Jacob. Not really. Despite being only a few feet away from him, I felt the distance between us was as wide as the Pacific Ocean, and I had no boat to traverse it.

"Have you ever thought you were one thing but you were really something else?" he asked.

I frowned. "Not really. I've always known I was going to run my parents' shop. Make floral arrangements, grow plants. I never doubted that."

"You're lucky, then." He said the words with such conviction that I wanted to ask him what he really meant. But then his expression grew shuttered, and I didn't have the courage to draw back the shades.

"Sorry," he said suddenly, "I didn't mean to get all vague and dramatic."

"It was basically the definition of vague-booking."

"I resent that. I don't even have a Facebook."

I knew that, because I paid attention to very important details like this. He had an Instagram, but he only updated it a few times a month. He used to have a Facebook, but he'd deactivated it years ago. But I kept that information to myself. There was no reason to prove to him I was, in fact, a total creep.

"Do you even like flowers?" I asked, curious. "You never seemed interested in your parents' place when we were kids."

"To be fair, I *was* just a kid."

"Yeah, but I've always loved the business. If I could spend all day with plants and avoid human contact, I would."

His lips twitched. "That's not necessarily a thing to brag about." His smile faded. "Would you believe me if I said that my parents never wanted me to run the business?"

I didn't believe him. Considering he was their only child, it didn't make sense that they'd been the ones resistant, not Jacob.

"Why not? Isn't that what parents want, for their kids to continue their legacy?" I said.

"My parents started Flowers with the idea that it would get successful enough to sell it and my parents would retire by the time they were in their fifties. When that didn't happen and my dad had a stroke, I basically had to threaten them to let me take over everything."

I stared at him in surprise. "I had no idea."

"You wouldn't have. My dad keeps any details of the business under lock and key. He wouldn't even tell *me* about it at first." Jacob sighed. "Now everything is complicated. I have to untangle the mess my parents made…"

I'd had no idea that Flowers was struggling. Then again, Jacob hadn't said as much, just that his parents were total control freaks. I could hear my dad's voice in my head, *Just like a West.*

"So does that mean you do care about plants?" I said. "Because it got lost in there."

"I do, especially within the last two years." He crossed his arms and leaned against the window. It was a casual pose that made whatever it was we were doing more intimate. "I even grew some tomatoes on my porch last summer."

"Oh my God, you crazy person. Next you're going to tell me you're growing eggplants and zucchini like a nutter."

"Eggplants are the fucking worst. I would never grow poisonous sponges."

"Eggplants and I have a sordid history." When I realized what I'd just said about a phallic-shaped vegetable, I blushed to the roots of my hair. "Not *like* that. Get your mind out of the gutter."

He gave me a slow perusal, his eyes gleaming in the low light. "I guess there are lots of sides to you I don't know about."

"Yeah, no. Do you remember when we got into that fight with Tommy Hedrick? My mom punished me by not letting me grow tomatoes that summer. I had to eat so many eggplants instead."

"That sounds like something your parents would use as a punishment. Mine just took away my Ninja Turtles for a week."

I smiled, even though my mind turned to the fact that my parents had never liked the Wests because of a ridiculous rivalry between them. As far as I knew, Jacob's parents didn't like mine, either. We were Romeo and Juliet of the florist world, except Romeo didn't know I existed because he was still hung up on Rosalind.

"We were good friends, weren't we?" Jacob's voice was soft. "As kids, I mean."

Before I could ask him why he'd decided to end that friendship with the whole standing-me-up-for-prom thing, he looked out the window and said, "The city's changed so much since I left. Every time I come back, it's like I have to relearn it."

"You're a rare breed, though." He raised an eyebrow at my statement. "Because you came back. There aren't many born-and-bred Seattleites left. They've all gone off to other places. Or at the very least, moved down to Tacoma."

Jacob chuckled and shuddered. "Don't even say its name."

"Why? Will I summon it like Beetlejuice? Tacoma, Tacoma, Tacom—"

Jacob moved so fast that he was like a blur. He pressed his fingers to my mouth to stop my flow of words. My breath stuttered in my chest. His fingers were impossibly warm, and it was like that heat transferred to every inch of my body.

A moment passed, then another. Jacob had yet to move his fingers from my lips. Impulsively, I touched the tip of my tongue to his middle finger. His eyes darkened.

"You're playing with fire," he rasped, finally moving his hand away and allowing me to speak.

I knew he didn't mean the game we'd just been playing. The game had shifted—the lines had been redrawn. I didn't know how to play this game to begin with, and I felt completely out of my depth. I wished I could play it cool, or even better, close the distance between us and kiss him. Anna would know what to do. Me, however? I always overthought things until it was too late.

I finally found my voice. "Would it be cheesy to say that I wouldn't mind getting burned? If we're continuing with this whole fire metaphor."

"Everyone should consent before any fires are lit," was his reply as he took my hand and kissed my palm. I froze when I felt his tongue lick a circle in the center of it. "It's only right," he added.

"Right. So right. People should always try to be right."

His other hand drifted down my back until he could pull me closer. When our bodies aligned, my breasts against his hard chest, the only thought in my mind was that Jacob West was going to kiss me and I really, really hoped I didn't fuck it all up.

He tilted my head back slightly before he leaned down to press his lips to mine. The kiss was soft, like a petal against the skin, but it only whet my appetite further. I wondered if I should open my mouth, or should I wait for him? Why was I such a mess?

"You're thinking too hard," he murmured, his breath warm. "Just enjoy yourself."

"Why do people always say shit like that? That just makes me think harder."

"Then I'll have to try harder to make you stop thinking."

I wanted to wish him Godspeed and good luck, until he kissed me again, angling his mouth so he could kiss me more deeply than before. This kiss wasn't gentle at all: it was possessive and wet and I felt the stroke of his tongue like a stroke against my clit. I moaned, clutching at his shoulder. When I felt his cock press against my belly, my pussy throbbed. I wanted to climb all over him. I wanted him never to stop kissing me. Mostly, I wanted him to touch me everywhere.

He kneaded my ass, lifting me so he could rub his hardness in the notch between my thighs. My toes curled. I wondered wildly if I could come just from this. I was already tight, achy. Desperate. My nipples were hardened nubs that, with every brush of his chest against mine, throbbed even more.

I'd never been kissed like this in my entire life. I'd almost convinced myself these feelings, these sensations, didn't exist. They existed in fiction and nowhere else. But Jacob put proof to that lie within a few strokes of his tongue against mine. I kept arching and rubbing against him like a cat. It was like I was trying to climb out of my very skin.

At this point, the only reason I hadn't collapsed at his feet was because he was holding me up. I was entirely at his disposal.

"Did it work?" he said finally. He licked at the pulse point in my neck.

"What worked?" I was totally dazed.

His smile made my pussy clench. "There's my answer, then."

He looked so cocky and smug that if I weren't so very horny I'd tell him to go fuck himself. Except I wanted him to fuck *me*. I wanted him to carry me into my bedroom, strip off my clothes, and plunge his cock into me until I screamed. I'd never wanted any man like I wanted Jacob right this moment.

I was about to wrap myself around him like a deranged octopus when Kevin yowled and launched himself at Jacob's ankle. Jacob yelled, I yelled, Kevin yelled. Jacob managed to boot Kevin off of him without damaging the stupid cat further, and I wanted to die of mortification.

Of course, whatever moment we'd been enjoying was broken. "Are you okay?" I asked.

"Fine." To my surprise, Jacob started laughing. "I think everything concerning you is trying to kill me tonight."

Kevin had run back to my room, the coward. "I've never seen Kevin do that. Maybe it's because you're a guy and he hasn't been around men?"

I could've bitten my tongue in half and swallowed it. Jacob didn't miss what I'd implied. The heat in his eyes disappeared, and suddenly, he was just the mysterious man who'd returned from New York and nothing else.

"I should go," he said. He looked like he was about to say something else, then shook his head. He murmured goodbye and that was that.

CHAPTER NINE

M ari held up a pink peony and a white one. "Which do you like better?"

"What is this for again?" I said.

Mari sighed. "For my bouquet. Pink or white? My dress is white so I thought pink, but I kind of like the idea of having all the flowers be white, too."

A few days after that mind-blowing kiss with Jacob, Mari invited me to her place to help her with wedding planning. Kate had joined us as well, although she was busy studying for an exam. I didn't know how she managed to concentrate while Mari and I talked bouquets, but Kate had always had a remarkable ability to retain information with little effort. I was surprised she was even studying at all.

"Neither," I said finally. I began to sketch a bouquet in pencil. "Since your bridesmaids are wearing pink, it'll be pink overload if your bouquets are pink, too."

Mari nibbled her bottom lip. "That's true."

I glanced at the color selection that Mari had chosen, my brain putting together arrangements and discarding them just as quickly. Mari watched me draw the bouquet in silence, and soon, Kate joined us and looked over my shoulder.

"Do you have markers or colored pencils?" I asked. "I should've brought mine."

Mari brought me some fine-tipped markers. If the whole Jacob thing hadn't totally scrambled my brain, I would've remembered to bring my sketchpad and markers that I used when drawing arrangements and bouquets for clients.

As I colored in the flowers, I thought again of Jacob's voice, roughened from kissing me. The way his hands had traveled over my body, pleasure blooming with every brush of his fingers against me. He hadn't tried contacting me in the last five days, and there'd been no stops at Buds and Blossoms. I'd tried not to let it hurt my feelings, but I'd be a liar if I said I wasn't mystified by the sudden cold shoulder. Had I said something stupid? Had I freaked him out when I'd admitted there hadn't been any guys at my apartment? I'd racked my brain to figure out what I could've done to make him run in the other direction, but even with Anna's help, we hadn't been able to think of a reason.

The bouquet drawing seemed to pour from my brain, through my fingers, without any conscious thought. One moment it was just a pencil sketch; the next, it was a bouquet of dark pink peonies, royal purple anemones and pale green dusty miller, along with navy blue feathers. "Since your wedding is in the evening and going to be in October, I think this will go perfectly. But I can change whatever you want."

Kate leaned over me, her hair brushing my cheek. "What flowers are those?"

I snorted and patted her head. "Go back to studying, you black thumb, you."

"It's not my fault plants die around me. They just don't like me. It's pretty. I like it. What about you, Mari?"

Mari took the sketch and looked at it for a long moment. I worried that she'd think the colors were too bright: she tended to gravitate more toward neutrals and pink. Then again, she had chosen maroon as one of her wedding colors.

"I love it," she finally pronounced. "I wouldn't have thought of using anemones. It's way better than I was thinking."

"Oh thank God," said Kate. "Because if you would've made me carry a boring pink bouquet as a bridesmaid, I'd hate you forever."

"Kate, bridesmaids are supposed to grin and bear it," I said.

Mari wrinkled her nose. "Why did I let you be in my wedding again?"

"Because you love me." Kate returned to her perch on Mari's overstuffed chair, her legs crossed and a pencil soon dangling from her mouth.

"She's a menace," I said. "I'm still not convinced we're related to her."

"You're a menace, too. Remember the time you put ragweed in my backpack as a prank, and it was covered in bugs?"

"Oh yeah." I smiled. "You were so mad at me. You wouldn't talk to me for a week."

Mari leaned back in her chair. "Didn't Jacob West help you get all that ragweed?" she said slyly.

I'd told Mari about Jacob's stopping by the shop, but nothing beyond that. I wasn't sure she would understand; Mari had never struggled for male attention. The thought of admitting that Jacob had kissed me and then had ghosted on me was humiliating.

"Did he?" I said, knowing full well that he had. That had been when we'd still been young enough to be friends. "I can't remember."

"You liar. I also know you aren't telling me everything. Besides, you're as red as a tomato right now. Either tell me, or I'm going to sic Kate on you."

I glanced over at Kate. She had her headphones on, and she was too busy studying to notice us. But if she so much as sniffed any kind of gossip about her sisters, she'd be like a bloodhound on the hunt. Except she was a little bloodhound with skinny arms and legs and a propensity to eat too many potato chips during the day. Although Kate was technically an adult now at nineteen, she was still our baby sister who'd followed me and Mari around all the time. She'd probably always be a kid in my mind, even when she was sixty-five.

"You wouldn't dare," I said, calling Mari's bluff. "You wouldn't want Kate to know the same time as you."

"To get you to spill, I'd do it." She looked over my shoulder. "Kate!"

"For the love of God, Mari." I slapped my hand over her mouth.

Kate called, "Did you say my name?"

"No!" I replied before Mari could. "Go back to studying."

Kate frowned, dubious, but she put her headphones back in after a moment. I grabbed Mari by the wrist and dragged her to her bedroom. I shut the door behind us and said in a rush, "I kissed Jacob West. Or really, he kissed me."

Mari's eyes widened into saucers. "Are you serious right now?"

"Do I sound like I'm kidding?"

"When did this happen? Wait, how did this happen? Have you been hanging out with him? Are you guys *dating?*" She started cackling like a witch. "Mom and Dad are going to freak out. They're going to lock you up in the basement!"

"We don't have a basement. This is Seattle, not Kansas."

"Then they'll lock you in a closet. Or under the house. If Dad doesn't blow the house up when he finds out." Mari gripped my shoulders. "Do you know what this means?"

"Honestly, at this point, your guess is as good as mine."

"It means that we could finally end this stupid feud between us. Then we wouldn't have to hear Dad talk about how much those Wests annoy him at every Thanksgiving! Dani, you have to lock this down. Poke a hole in the condom. Get pregnant, make him marry you."

"Good lord, is that what you did to get David to propose?"

Mari had the audacity to look offended. "Of course not. He *loves* me. And I'm not pregnant."

Now I was irritated. "So the only way Jacob would stay with me is if I got pregnant? That's nice of you to say."

Mari finally realized what she'd said, and she winced. "No, no. I was joking. Mostly joking. I do think this could be good for both families." Her expression darkened. "Unless you break up. Please don't break up. I couldn't take it. Dad would probably burn the Wests' house down. He wouldn't survive in prison. You can't grow orchids there, you know."

I rolled my eyes and moved further into her bedroom. The quilt was off-white, the furniture a deep walnut. The only color was a crimson amaryllis in the window. It smelled like my sister: sweet pea and vanilla. Looking at the bed, I wondered how she managed to keep her quilt clean if she and

David were having sex all the time in her bed. Which was not an image I needed in my brain at all. I wasn't sure if the thought of my sister having sex or the idea of Prius-driving David humping her was worse. He probably orgasmed at the thought of his stock options increasing.

"We aren't dating," I said to the amaryllis.

"But you said he kissed you."

I shrugged, even though I felt my heart splinter. "It was just one kiss, Mari. Not a marriage proposal."

"Men don't kiss women unless they at least want to sleep with you."

"I think it was just the thrill of the moment. A throwaway thing. Maybe an experiment." I touched the delicate petals of the amaryllis. "I don't know. I wish I could ask him, but who wants a guy to tell them they'd rather not kiss you again, thank you very much?"

Mari frowned. She sat down on her bed, peering at me. "You know what you should do?"

"Give up on men forever and live in a spinster commune that rescues senior cats?"

"No, you should talk to him. Like an adult. If you like him, you should tell him as much."

I'd rather stab my eyeballs with a spork. I'd rather eat a bowl of sporks. I'd rather watch David hump my sister in this very bed, which said a lot about my current mental state.

"No, thanks," I said instead.

"You were totally in love with Jacob when we were younger. But you never said anything, did you? You just stared at him from afar and hoped he could read your mind."

"Um, are you forgetting when I asked him to prom? And then he *stood me up*?" Those feelings of humiliation and anger rose up inside me again. I was glad of them, because they reminded me why falling for Jacob was a bad idea in the first place. Yeah, we were adults now, but that didn't erase his betrayal, either. It still didn't help me trust him now.

"To be fair, he was a seventeen-year-old boy," said Mari, folding her hands primly in her lap.

"That's no excuse. And seventeen is almost eighteen, and eighteen is legally an adult."

"We both know that eighteen doesn't mean anything in terms of maturity. Pretty sure you were still watching *SpongeBob SquarePants* when you turned eighteen."

I pointed a finger at her, my other hand covering my heart. "The first four seasons of *SpongeBob* are brilliant and it's not my fault you can't see that."

"Now you're just deflecting. And about a cartoon sponge who lives in a pineapple." Mari's tone was dry. Her tone became gentler as she added, "What's the worst that can happen if you're honest with him?"

He could tell me it was a mistake to kiss me. He could tell me he isn't really attracted to me. I could burst into flames from sheer embarrassment. He could break my heart a second time.

"I'll consider it," I said, even though both Mari and I knew how stubborn I could be. She'd always been able to share her feelings easily. She would go up to boys in grade school, tell them point-blank that she liked them, and then she'd have a boyfriend. But she'd never faced rejection, either. She didn't know what it was like to love and have that love not embraced but pushed to the side like an inconvenience.

It was easier, I knew, to keep everything inside of me instead of risking more heartbreak. Besides, I was *busy*.

"This conversation really isn't passing the Bechdel test," I said. "We need to talk about our careers. Feminism. The male gaze. The pros and cons of hybrid vehicles. Something."

"David just bought a new hybrid."

I groaned. As I looked at Mari through my fingers, I noticed the plastic button sitting on Mari's bedside table. There was another one on the other side, too. They looked like something out of a game. I went over and picked one up, flipping it over.

"Is this a light?" I pressed it, but it didn't do anything.

"Don't touch that!" Mari was beet-red and grabbed the button from me.

"What, did I just press the button to launch nuclear warheads?"

"Worse." Mari moaned. "You just told David I want to have sex with him."

It was such an absurd answer that I started laughing, thinking she was kidding, when I quickly realized she wasn't. She glared at me so hard that I could feel a hole in my shirt burning.

"I'm so confused," I said.

She lifted her chin. "It's none of your business, but David isn't so great about initiating love-making. He found these buttons that we use instead. If a person wants to have sex, they hit the button. But if the other person doesn't, no one is rejected."

My lip wobbled from trying not to laugh like a crazy person. Mari looked so serious about talking about these sex buttons that I had to chew on the inside of my cheeks to keep from laughing. "You can't just tell each other?" I croaked.

"You wouldn't understand because you've never dated anyone." Mari's words were like a whiplash.

I reared backward, stung. "Maybe not, but I know that in an adult relationship, you use your words. Not some plastic buttons."

Mari's anger faded as soon as it had emerged. "I'm sorry. I shouldn't have said that." She set the button down, her expression abashed. "It's embarrassing, isn't it? I wish we had the type of sex life where David just threw me over his shoulder and had his wicked way with me."

I didn't really want to have this conversation about my sister's sex life, but she seemed so forlorn now, sitting on her bed, that I couldn't not help her in some way.

"I think you really should talk to him," was my only answer.

"I have. He tells me that I reject him too much." She wrinkled her nose. "I only tell him no because I'm exhausted from work, or I'm on my period, or he's sweaty from his stupid Pilates class—"

"So it's more of a timing issue."

"Exactly. This way, we can get over that issue but nobody's feelings are hurt."

I searched her face. "Mari, why are you marrying him? He's basically the human equivalent of cardboard."

I knew I'd overstepped when her eyes sparked with rage. Standing up, she said, "He is not. He's a good man. And you don't get to lecture me about my life, considering you make out with guys who then totally ghosts on you."

"Then don't ask me my advice!"

"Did I say I needed your advice?"

We didn't hear the bedroom door creak open until Kate said, "If you guys are going to beat each other up, there's more room in the living room than in here."

I stared at Kate; Mari stared at Kate; Mari and I stared at each other. Then I said, "Katherine Lydia, were you listening at the door?"

Kate shrugged. "You guys were getting loud." She went over to the nightstand and began to hit the other button, grinning like the evil brat she was. "If you hit the button a bunch of times in a row, does that mean you want to do anal?"

Mari blushed scarlet. I started laughing so hard I was crying.

And Kate just said, "Well, it's a valid question."

CHAPTER TEN

The second time I fell in love with Jacob, I was thirteen.
That isn't to say I'd fallen *out* of love with him at any point between five and thirteen. It was just that he gave me another reason to love him. It was like he kept adding dandelions to my pile of love for him and then metaphorically making me tons of flower crowns with them.

By eighth grade, Jacob was the golden boy of our junior high. He was, literally, golden: golden hair, golden skin. Every time he smiled, his teeth sparkled like out of some toothpaste commercial. I swear a theme song played in my head anytime he walked past me—that theme song being the saxophone solo from "Careless Whisper." Every. Damn. Time. I heard that stupid saxophone in my brain when I saw Jacob.

"Do you think he ever smells bad?" I asked Anna.

It was two days before Valentine's Day, aka the worst day ever when you didn't have a boyfriend. Which was me. I had no boyfriend. Not even Tommy would date somebody like me, and that was saying something. I was all frizzy hair and braces and my locker had plants growing inside it. Apparently, boys didn't think that was cool.

Anna wrinkled her nose. "He's a boy. I'm sure his room smells like sweaty balls." Considering Anna had two older brothers, she was probably right, but I wanted to believe he never so much as farted. He was perfect. He could do nothing wrong.

"Why don't you tell him you like him for once?" said Anna. She raised a black eyebrow. Already curvy, Anna was womanly where I was the opposite. She said she hated it, because it gave her more attention than she wanted. I told her it couldn't be worse than being as flat as a board like me.

It was one of the many things we commiserated on, along with how dumb boys were, how cute boys were, and how annoying it was when Mrs. Turner spit when she got really excited about geometric proofs. Anna and I imagined that Mrs. Turner went home and wrote sonnets to her favorite proofs, along with odes to parallelograms. She really had a thing for those, too.

"Why would I tell him that I liked him?" I slammed my locker door shut. "He's just going to say no. So what's the point?"

"You don't know that."

Considering Jacob's last girlfriend was Tiffany McClain (yes, that Tiffany)—a cheerleader and one of the most popular girls in school—the likelihood of Jacob wanting to date *me* was laughable.

"Jacob's nice," insisted Anna as we walked to class. "He's not like the other guys."

I sighed. No, Jacob was nice—too nice. He held doors

open for girls; he made sure everyone was invited to his parties. I was pretty sure he wasn't actually a human boy, because every other one I'd met was smelly, rude, and liked to draw penises on the back of your neck during class.

Right then, I saw Jacob walking toward his locker. He had study hall this period—yes, I knew his schedule; no, it wasn't creepy—and he nodded at me and Anna. I ducked my head and avoided eye contact as I scuttled to class.

Jacob West was never going to give me a necklace at a birthday party. I had accepted that. It was fine. I was a dandelion amongst roses and lilies and I couldn't change that anymore than you could change the species of a flower.

"Hey, Dani, wait up," called Jacob. He jogged up to us. He pushed his bangs from his forehead and smiled that damn smile. I heard "Careless Whisper" playing in my mind. When he brushed his hair from his face, I always saw it in slow motion.

Oh God, was he going to ask me to be his valentine? Was Anna right? My heart thudded in my chest, and blood rushed to my cheeks.

I felt Anna elbow me. "Dani, did you hear him? Do you have the notes for World History?"

Jacob smiled apologetically. "I missed it since we had an away game. I know you take the best notes out of everyone."

He wanted my notes. Of course he wanted my notes. He wasn't going to be giving me chocolate and balloons and a teddy bear. Scrambling inside my binder, I pulled out my very meticulous notes and handed them to him. "Here you go. Let me know if you need anything else."

"You're the coolest. Thanks."

Anna frowned at his retreating figure. "You guys used to be friends. Like, you played together. I remember I'd find you playing in his backyard."

"Yeah, so what?"

She shrugged. "Just wondered what happened."

"We grew up. That's all."

THE NEXT DAY, I braced myself. Pink and red balloons were taped to lockers, while I heard girls giggle as they ripped open valentines. When I got to my locker, I was shocked to see a valentine taped to it. I peeled it off, squinting at the handwriting. Had Anna gotten me one?

"What's that?" said Anna over my shoulder.

Well, never mind that assumption. I opened the small, white envelope to find a pink ladybug card inside. In sparkly letters, it read *I'm buggy for you!* Turning over the card, I saw the words I'd dreamed about for so long but had never imagined would happen.

Dani, you're a cool girl. I like you. Come sit with me at lunch. Jacob.

I let out such a loud squeal that Anna clapped her hands over her ears.

"Look! He likes me!" I shoved the card into Anna's face.

She took it, read it, her eyes widening. "Wow."

I leaned against my locker, sighing with happiness. I took the card from Anna and kissed it before placing it in a safe spot on the top shelf, where my latest plant was also growing. It was a philodendron that didn't mind the darkness of an eighth grader's locker.

"I can't believe it. Do you really think he sent you this?" said Anna.

"Seriously?" I slammed my locker closed. "Weren't you the one telling me to confess my feelings?"

"Yeah, I mean…" She nibbled on her lower lip. "It just… doesn't seem like him, that's all."

I didn't care. Jacob West liked *me*, and I was going to sit with him at lunch. Maybe we'd hold hands between classes. My heart flipped inside my chest at the thought. It was too good to be true—but I wanted it to be true so badly that I didn't want to consider any other possibility.

I had only one class with Jacob before lunch. I sat in the back, so I could only stare at him longingly. He didn't look my way, which I attributed to him wanting to keep things on the down-low until lunch. I was fine with that. I'd rather make a splashy announcement where everyone could see us.

When lunch arrived, I entered the cafeteria with sweaty palms and a racing heart. The cafeteria was packed with students, the smells of chicken nuggets and burnt microwavable lunches filling the air. I wasn't even hungry.

"There's Jacob," I whispered to Anna.

"Wait, Dani—"

I didn't hear her. I pushed past a group of seventh graders, making a beeline to Jacob's usual table. I watched him for a moment with his guy friends. He was laughing at something someone said, his head tipped back. He'd just gotten his braces off and his perfectly straight teeth made him seem older, more mature.

"Jacob," I said breathlessly. There was just enough space to his left that I managed to slip in and sit next to him. "Hi," was all I could manage.

The boys across from me looked at each other in confusion. I never sat with them. The only people who sat at this table were Jacob, his guy friends, and whichever girl Jacob was dating.

But I was now that girl. Finally.

"What are you doing?" Connor Hall asked me. "Are you lost?"

Next to him, Kenny Martin snorted and coughed out a laugh.

A blush climbed up my cheeks, but I ignored them. I took the valentine from my pocket and said shyly, "I got your card. Thank you."

Confusion clouded Jacob's face. He looked at the card in my hand and said, "What?"

Fear congealed in my gut. Kenny and Connor started laughing across from me. Across the cafeteria, I saw Tiffany smile at me, but it wasn't a nice smile. She and her friends were watching us, and they kept giggling.

They'd pranked me, I realized. Jacob had never sent me a valentine. They'd just wanted to mess with me. Tears sprang to my eyes. I was about to get up and find the nearest bathroom to cry in, when Jacob said, "Oh, right. You're welcome, Dani." He slung an arm around my shoulder and shot a pointed look at his two friends. "Dani's going to eat lunch with us today. Got it?"

Kenny and Connor shrugged. Connor whispered something to Kenny, but I didn't care. I gazed up at Jacob, the warm weight of his arm on my shoulder, and I fell so much in love with him it was physically painful.

I took that valentine home and placed it inside the shoebox where the dried-up flower wreath Jacob had given me in kindergarten was stored. I didn't care that the handwriting was Tiffany's. It had become another memory to cherish. I placed the card inside, like it was an offering at a temple, and pushed the box deep under my bed, where it stayed for the next four years.

CHAPTER ELEVEN

I hadn't been able to figure out my own dilemma by the time I joined Anna that evening, a week after that kiss with Jacob. She had the rare night off, and we went to a fancy new bar only a few blocks from her apartment. During the day it was a coffee house that served deconstructed lattes (because of course it did), but at night it turned into a fancy cocktail restaurant that served things like deconstructed avocado toast. It was just an avocado that you had to peel yourself and a piece of bread on a wooden cutting board that cost $20.

I was well into my third cocktail, feeling the delicious buzz of alcohol, when I bemoaned, "I'm a mess, Anna."

"We all are. But don't blame yourself because Jacob left you high and dry. Well, not really. He left you wet and cock-blocked." She snickered.

"I'm never going to get a guy to pop my cherry at this rate." I stared at my martini, mostly hypnotized by the preserved lemon curl floating in the liquid. I wondered if I could eat it. Pulling it out of my drink, I dropped it into my mouth, grimacing immediately at the bitterness. Yeah, maybe that hadn't been the best idea I'd ever had.

"Aw, honey, it'll happen." Anna took my hands and squeezed them. "And if I were gay, I'd pop your cherry so hard you wouldn't be able to walk for a week."

"You're so sweet." I felt near tears at that random declaration. "You know I'd sleep with you in a heartbeat," I cried.

"I know." Anna held up her empty cocktail glass. "Another one, bartender! And for my friend, too!"

I knew I should probably tell Anna I was going home, but then I finished off my third martini in one gulp and decided that would be a dumb idea. I hadn't driven here, anyway. I'd walk home, or take the bus. Maybe both. Could you walk on top of the bus? For some reason, that thought was hilarious to me, and I started giggling uncontrollably.

Well into our fourth drinks, Anna began to lean over the counter and proposition the bartender. He was handsome, in a "I got a degree in philosophy and now bartend to pay the bills" kind of way. When he seemed uninterested in Anna's suggestive comments, she pointed to me. "What do you think about my friend? Isn't she gorgeous?"

The bartender looked like he'd rather be at the bottom of Elliott Bay. "She's gorgeous," he deadpanned.

"I don't believe you!" Anna turned to me. "He's a jerk. Don't listen to him."

"I said she was gorgeous," said the bartender.

"But you didn't *mean* it!"

Soon Anna and the bartender were in a heated debate, and I was considering going home. I was tired. I needed to scoop Kevin's litter, otherwise he'd pee in my bed for skipping a day. I wondered if Jacob had to worry about things like scooping cat shit. I doubted he had a cat, but metaphorically speaking.

Jacob had always seemed above normal things like litter boxes or putting gas in his car or going to Walgreens for toilet paper. He probably didn't need toilet paper. He was too perfect for something so banal.

A small part of my brain was telling me that I was very drunk and that I should stop drinking. That small part kept shrinking, but it was there, all the same.

"I need to go home!" I said to Anna. "Let's go."

I walked—more like stumbled—to Anna's place, where she tried to get me to stay the night. But I needed to go home to Kevin. He had a litter box. It was very important. I told her I'd take the bus, except that it was late enough that I'd have to wait at least a half hour, if not longer, to catch one.

"Fine, you whore." Anna hugged me and gave me a sloppy kiss. "I love you. Be safe."

I began to walk home, but it was a slow walk. I kept getting distracted by the cracks in the sidewalk. I laughed when I saw a raccoon dart into a dumpster behind a restaurant. I watched another raccoon join it, and I stood there for who knew how long, enjoying the way the animals pilfered around in the trash to find something edible. I wondered what it would be like to live in a dumpster. It seemed like it could be cozy, if you really wanted it to be.

I didn't remember walking up the hill to my street. I felt a little sick to my stomach, but mostly thirsty from both the walk and the alcohol. My head was starting to hurt.

As I passed by a row of brand-new apartments, I

wondered if Jacob lived in them. He said he lived about three blocks from me, right? He hadn't said that he'd bought a house, and the majority of this neighborhood was homes with a few condos and one apartment complex like mine. I leaned on the fence outside this complex, mostly because I was dizzy, but also because I really wanted to see if Jacob would come to the window like some pantomime of *Romeo and Juliet.*

"Jacob, wherefore art thou, Jacob?" I singsonged. "Deny thy father and, something, something, Capulet, but you aren't a Capulet, you're a *West.*" I moaned. "Why did you have to be born a West? We could've had it all!"

I started singing "Rollin' in the Deep" as best as I could, which was not good at all when I was sober, let alone drunk. After a few earsplitting bars, a man yelled from his window, "Shut the fuck up, lady!"

"You shut the fuck up!" I yelled back. I was about to fight this guy when someone clasped my elbow to pull me back from the brink.

"What are you—?" It was Jacob. He did live here. I'd been right! "You heard me!"

Jacob's lips twitched. "Me and everyone in Seattle. How drunk are you right now?"

I stumbled, but Jacob's grip tightened to keep me from falling. "Not remotely drunk," I slurred.

"Yeah, no. Come on. I'm walking you home."

"You don't know where I live!"

"I was at your apartment, Dani."

I wrinkled my nose at him. I didn't want to think about him in my apartment because he'd kissed me and then he'd gone AWOL on me like the big Jerkface McJerkson he was.

"You suck," was what I could come up with after a block of silent walking.

Jacob glanced at me, his eyes creased. "Yeah, I know."

"So you're admitting it."

"Isn't that what I just said?"

I poked him in the chest. "You kiss me, and then you act like I died. Who does that? Did someone send you a fake funeral invite, Jacob West? Did a dead girl catfish you and claim it was me? Huh?" With every word, I poked him in the chest. He didn't make a move to stop me.

"It's complicated."

"Why don't you marry that Facebook status, butt-face? Since you love it so much."

I almost fell into a rhododendron bush, but once again, Jacob caught me. My knight in shining armor. I still hated him, because he never failed to turn my entire life upside down and I was tired of it.

When we got to my apartment, I didn't want him to go. Not because I wanted him to kiss me again, but because I wanted answers. We stood in a dark corner under the stairs to my apartment, and I couldn't make out Jacob's expression now.

"Why did you kiss me?" I demanded. "Why? Were you just messing with me?"

I pushed at his shoulder, but he caught my hands and held them tightly. Not enough to hurt, but enough to show me that he was stronger than me.

"I told myself that I'd leave you alone." He sounded... anguished. Why would he be anguished? It made no sense.

"Well, you're doing a great job of it. Walking me home.

Kissing me. Feeling me up. Wow, you should get an award for how good you're doing at this whole thing. You know what, Jacob? Go eat a bag of musty dicks. I'm done."

I tried to pull away, but he moved so I was forced against the opposite wall. He pressed his body against mine, and I felt the air whooshing from my lungs. I wasn't sure anyway if it was the alcohol or him that was making me so dizzy.

"You don't understand. I never wanted this to happen." His words were a heated whisper against my ear. "It wasn't supposed to happen."

Despite his words, his lips traced a path down my throat. I shuddered. I felt his hardness against my belly. At the very least, he still desired me. I felt triumph fill me. He could tell himself whatever he wanted: his body wasn't lying.

He licked my throat. He'd let go of my hands, but I didn't want to break free of him. I wanted to wrap myself around him; I wanted him to possess every inch of me. I was so hot— from his presence, his mouth, the alcohol.

"I can't get enough of you," he said roughly. "I want to touch every inch of you."

I quivered. So much for his saying *this couldn't happen.* It seemed to be happening regardless.

The alcohol made me more daring than ever: I touched his chest and moved downward until I cupped the length of his cock. He hissed out a breath.

"Come upstairs," I said. Because I was brazen, and drunk, and desperate for him.

He stilled. I wondered if he was considering my offer when he pushed off of me. Cool air rushed between us, and suddenly I felt very cold.

"This can't happen," he said, his chest heaving.

I moved closer to him. I dug my fingers into his shirt and held on, because the world was tilting with alarming speed.

And although the words that I thought were, *I want you,* I didn't get to say them because, suddenly, I was vomiting only inches from Jacob's shoes.

CHAPTER TWELVE

Normally I enjoyed driving to Vancouver, but today had not been enjoyable. Not only had I gotten stuck in traffic on I-5, which doubled my travel time, but I realized after a half hour that I'd forgotten the box of brochures for Buds and Blossoms that I'd needed to bring. I'd told Judith and Will, our other employee, that I needed everything put together that afternoon, but Will had been out with the flu and Judith had been frazzled and distracted, so all my plans and instructions had gone to hell with alarming speed.

By the time I crossed the border and got to the hotel, I was starving, sweaty from stress, and exhausted. I wanted to order room service, take a hot bath, and call it a night so I could function like a human being tomorrow.

When I entered the hotel lobby and saw the wide shoulders, the golden hair, the tight ass, I didn't need to wonder who it was. I wasn't remotely surprised that Jacob was here. I'd often attended conventions like this with my dad, and the Wests were often present as well. Running the same type of businesses tended to throw people together.

Did I go back to my car, wait for Jacob to check in and go to his room, or did I act like an adult and get in line behind him? I hadn't spoken to him since I'd thrown myself at him and then puked on his shoes. It wasn't exactly the greatest way to get a guy to chase after you, apparently.

I had just about decided to hightail it back to my car when I heard Jacob say, "Are you serious right now?"

Curiosity killed the cat. I moved closer, my ears pricked as the hotel employee replied, "I'm so sorry, Mr. West, but it looks like we don't have any record of your reservation. Let me go get my manager to see what we can do."

Jacob sighed, his face tight. He looked like he could cheerfully strangle someone, and I couldn't blame him. Suddenly all my frustration with him, my confusion, my physical attraction to him that was all tangled up like a knotted ball of yarn, melted away in the face of this. He looked as tired as I was, and considering the hotel had sold out of rooms for this conference ages ago, I doubted they had an extra room for him.

Finally he spotted me. I gave him an awkward little wave, and promptly felt like an idiot for *waving*. Who did that when you were only three feet from each other?

I was saved from further painful conversation when I went up to the counter to check in. I heard the last of Jacob's conversation with the manager, and I heard something about a voucher for another hotel.

I didn't think about the consequences when I went over to where he was sitting, his phone to his ear. Who knew if it was out of altruism or selfishness. Or maybe I was just a complete masochist. The world may never really know.

He'd just hung up and was dialing another number when I said, "You didn't get a room?"

"No. Apparently their computers ate my fucking reservation." He sighed. "I have a voucher, but there aren't any rooms available nearby. It wouldn't matter, except I didn't drive up here."

"You can room with me." At his surprised look, I added, "If you want. I even have a suite, so there's a sofa bed. Although I can sleep on that. It doesn't really matter. But we don't have to share a bed." I laughed, my brain automatically conjuring up images of us sharing a bed. Jacob would have his arms around me as he kissed down my body, his hair brushing my throat, my breasts, my stomach—

"I can't do that," he said, breaking my sex fantasy. "But I appreciate the offer."

"Sure, you can. It'll be fun. Like a slumber party. Except we aren't teenage girls. I promise not to make you play truth or dare." *Stop talking, Dani, please stop talking.*

He smiled, despite his sour mood. "I'll pay you for half of it, of course."

I hadn't even been thinking about payment, which said a lot about my current mental state. "That's fine."

By the time we reached our room, after Jacob had agreed and we'd gotten him his own hotel room key, I was a bundle of nerves. We'd be in the same hotel room, sharing a bathroom, getting dressed and undressed so close together. It would be like we were dating. Except we wouldn't be sharing a bed, or enjoying a shower together.

But I wouldn't throw myself at him again. He'd already made it clear nothing more could happen between us. Besides,

I needed to remember who he was: my direct competitor. But the more time I spent with him, the more I wanted to forget that annoying detail. Except *he* apparently couldn't ignore that detail, considering he'd told me this "thing" between us wasn't going to go beyond kisses and some heavy petting.

What a damn shame, I thought. I really enjoyed the heavy petting.

The suite consisted of a small living room with a sofa and television, while the bedroom had a queen-sized bed. After Jacob insisted that I take the bed while he slept on the sofa, I began to unpack.

I heard Jacob doing the same, and the moment felt so unbearably intimate that I could've come right out of my skin. I wondered what he wore to bed—boxers? pajamas? nothing? Surely he wouldn't go to bed naked with me around. I swallowed against the lump in my throat, my mouth going dry at the thought of seeing Jacob naked. God, he'd be naked when he took a shower. I'd be just feet away from him, water dripping down his body, his skin heated—

"Are you hungry?"

I'd been obsessing over this entire situation so much that I'd forgotten that I was starving. As if on cue, my stomach rumbled. "I could eat."

"Good. Let's go down to the hotel restaurant. I'm too tired to go find a place."

I smiled. "Agreed. Let me finish unpacking."

Was it dumb that I was pleased he'd invited me to eat dinner with him? Probably, but I didn't care.

To my surprise, Jacob didn't return to the living area. He leaned against the mantel, watching me. Well, I wasn't going to act like a big boob if he wanted to watch me put away my bra and panties. We weren't in eighth grade anymore where the thought of a boy seeing my bra strap sent me into a tailspin of embarrassment.

"I've been meaning to apologize for the other night," I said. "I hope I didn't ruin your shoes?"

He chuckled. "You missed my shoes. You only ruined the sidewalk, I'm afraid."

I blushed so hot that I felt like my face was on fire. "Oh my God," I moaned, covering my eyes. "I can't believe I did that. I never drink that much. I'm just sorry you had to see it."

"We're even now. Thanks again for sharing your room with me."

Through the gaps in between my fingers, I could see his expression turn serious. Why did he have to look so yummy in a gray button-up shirt, its sleeves rolled up his forearms, his eyes that deep blue you could drown in? It was rude. A girl couldn't think when a guy was as yummy as him. It was like my brain short-circuited from hormones. And he kept looking at me like that, like he wasn't sure if he thought I were insane or if he wanted to eat me up.

I turned away, hurrying to unpack. "Okay, I'm ready. Let me put my shoes on."

He moved toward me and reached down to pick something up. "You dropped this." A black, lace thong dangled from his finger. His smile was devilish now.

"Shit." I grabbed the thong and threw it into a drawer. Jacob laughed, the sound making my body heat. Christ, his laugh alone could make me wet and aching.

"Let's go before I do something even more embarrassing,"

I muttered. Jacob just laughed quietly the entire walk down to the restaurant.

IF THE UNIVERSE didn't want me to think this was a date with Jacob, then it really shouldn't have seated us in a nook nestled at the back of the restaurant. It was dangerous, that nook, because it gave us the illusion of privacy.

It was also tiny, and more than once we played accidental footsie underneath the table. By the third time, I was almost certain that Jacob was doing it on purpose.

"Tell me about New York," I said after we'd ordered.

"Anything in particular?"

"Whatever you want." I put my chin on my hands, smiling. "I want to hear about something that doesn't involve complaining about the Seattle Freeze, or all the bikes that the city just dropped on every corner, or the fact that the buses are never on time."

"So, what happens in every metro area?"

"Now you're just avoiding the question."

He sat back a little, considering what he was going to say. It had to have been difficult, uprooting his life to come back to the area. Even though Seattle was where he'd grown up, it didn't mean he considered it home.

"Tell me something no one else knows," I said.

His blue eyes sparkled. "Okay. After I graduated with my MBA, I worked in a flower shop."

I snorted. "Be serious. We all know you were this high-powered stockbroker person. Your parents told everyone—

even my parents, who aren't exactly big fans of your mom and dad."

"Oh, that happened eventually." Jacob swirled his whiskey neat in his glass. I had refrained from any alcohol for obvious reasons.

"But it was right after the stock market crashed, and I couldn't get a job to save my life. Even with my fancy connections from NYU and everything. I had a bright, shiny new degree but not a lick of work experience. So, I went back to my roots." He smiled. "Pun intended."

"How long did you work there?" I leaned forward, fascinated.

"For about a year, before one of my professors learned about how I was slumming it in the Bronx"—here Jacob snorted—"and basically got a job for me. I think he did it mostly because, if anyone found out one of the business school grads couldn't get a job, they'd look bad."

"That was…nice of him."

"That's one way to put it."

I couldn't help but look at Jacob in a new light. I'd always assumed he'd breezed through undergrad, then business school. That he'd had an easy, breezy life from the time he'd been born until this very night, sitting in a booth at a restaurant in Vancouver with me, the weird plant girl.

"So then you got your job, a fancy new apartment not in the Bronx," I supplied, "and you lived happily ever after?"

Jacob leaned back, assessing me. "I'd ask what you mean, but I think I already know."

"Oh, come on. Despite that one-year blip, you've had an easy life." I winced inwardly, but I kept going, because I'd started on this track. "You were the golden boy when we were growing up. Everyone liked you; everyone wanted to be you. You get into NYU and get out of Seattle. You get a great job, a great career. A great girlfriend, according to the gossip in the neighborhood. What else could you have wanted?"

Jacob smiled, but the warmth had left his eyes. "If we're still playing this game of 'never have I ever,' the girlfriend? She got a job in Wisconsin and didn't want to do a long-distance relationship. So we ended it."

"Oh. Were you sad about it?" I couldn't tell, based on his seemingly blasé expression.

"Are you asking if I was in love with her?"

"Well, yes. In a way."

"I thought I was, but then we broke up, and it wasn't a big deal." He shrugged. "My life isn't as dramatic as people would like to think it is."

It was a relief to think that he wasn't still longing for his ex-girlfriend, but at the same time, the fact that his heart wasn't easily touched was...concerning. Then again, some-times I couldn't tell what was bravado and what was the truth with him.

"I guess a lot of things in my life have been great," he allowed, "but what you've heard is probably not as exciting as the truth."

"So you're saying you're not as *substantial* as people think?" I bit back a grin.

He leaned toward me, his voice pitched low. "Now that would be a lie. Why do you think I've always been so popular? Everything about me is...substantial."

My cheeks heated. Despite admitting that he'd been "slumming it," as he put it, for a year, he still managed to keep his aplomb. He was still the sexiest man in the room. I'd be annoyed, if I weren't so attracted to him.

He kept tapping his fingers against his empty glass of whiskey. I remembered how his hands had touched me—more than once, now—how my nipples had hardened to almost painful points. Like they were doing right now. I crossed my legs, my pussy pulsing, and I swore I could see a flare of heat in Jacob's eyes.

"What about you?" he said, his voice like a caress. I barely restrained a shiver. "Tell me something no one else knows about you."

Before I could answer, the waitress brought our meals. My stomach rumbled, and I was so hungry I had to stop myself from shoveling the food down my throat. I had a feeling Jacob wouldn't keep looking at me like he wanted to eat *me* if I did that.

"Come on, you didn't answer my question," cajoled Jacob. "Fair is fair."

"Fine." I thought a moment, and then said, "Do you remember that dandelion wreath you made me in kindergarten?"

"Vaguely." He said the words, but he was suddenly very interested in his hamburger when he said them.

"Well, I kept it. For a long time, in a box under my bed."

"Really? What happened to it?"

I hadn't meant to lead us down this path, but maybe I'd wanted to, subconsciously. I took a bite of my salad to forestall my answer.

"I got rid of it on prom night." He looked up at me when I said the words. "Somebody stood me up."

He was silent for a long moment, and I almost wished I

hadn't said anything. Oh, I wanted answers—who wouldn't? But was it worth bringing up the past to destroy this *thing* that was blooming between us now?

"I was a selfish little ass-wipe back then." He sighed, shaking his head. "But that's not an excuse."

"No, not really." I swallowed hard against the lump in my throat. "What happened, exactly?"

He shrugged. "Tiffany and I had broken up two weeks before prom. I was pretty messed up over it. She was my first —" He smiled awkwardly. "You know what I mean. Then she shows up at my door that night, telling me she loved me and wanted to get back together. And we did. That's why I stood you up."

"I saw you two, you know. I saw you driving off with her."

Jacob grimaced. "Shit. Why are you even sitting here with me? You should've had the waitress poison my burger."

"Oh, don't think I didn't consider it. Sadly, it's apparently against the law to poison someone in Canada. Maybe when we're back in Seattle."

"For what it's worth, I'm sorry. Even if it's nine years too late."

"Thank you." I poked at my salad. "Honestly, you also taught me a valuable lesson, so I guess I should thank you for that, too."

He cocked an eyebrow. "Really? I find that hard to believe."

"I realized that people will always let you down in the end. That when you trust somebody without reservation, you're going to get hurt. I was glad to get the lesson out of the way by the time I got to college."

"Because you've never let anyone down?" His voice was hard.

"Of course I have. Everyone does, because we're all human. I've fucked up so many times…" I stabbed at my salad, thinking of every time I'd disappointed my parents, my dad especially. "I'm not perfect."

"So you let yourself be imperfect, but when someone else messes up, that's it? It's over? That person is dead to you?"

"I never said that. Now you're just putting words in my mouth."

Jacob took a drink of his second whiskey. I watched in fascination as his throat worked, the way his Adam's apple bobbed. Even when he was pissed at me, I wanted him. What kind of sickness was that, anyway?

"You know what I think, Dandelion?"

I stilled. No one but my parents called me by my full name because I hated that name. It reminded me of the fact that I was named after a weed people always tried to eradicate from their lawns.

"I think that it's easier for you to write people off, because then you can never get hurt. If they fuck up, well, that's it. You can move on. But you know what'll happen to you in the end?"

My voice wobbled. "What?"

"You'll end up alone. Since, like you said, nobody is perfect."

"Maybe I like being alone."

Jacob's smile was sad. "Nobody wants to be alone, sweetheart."

I hardly remembered returning to our room that evening. Neither of us finished our food, although I took mine to go, thinking that maybe I'd get hungry again. Only if this lead weight in my stomach ever decided to go away, though, based on the way it seemed to grow larger as I listened to Jacob move about the living area, or how he barely glanced my way as he went into the bathroom, it wasn't going anywhere any time soon.

CHAPTER THIRTEEN

I 'd long since realized that plant people were all, collectively, a little strange. At conventions like this one, it was as if their strangeness was amplified tenfold. Suddenly it was perfectly socially acceptable to thrust a sample of soil macro-biotics in someone's face, or wax poetic on the best kinds of rakes or shovels.

I had a small booth where I was selling a variety of flower bulbs that we grew in our greenhouse: tulip, dahlia, and peony bulbs. Although we didn't have a huge selection, people recognized our store and knew that our bulbs were some of the best in the state. I wondered if I was going to sell out before the convention was even over, which would be great, but also a little awkward since there was still one more day after this one.

I was glad of the distraction of people wearing shirts that said things like *I'm so excited I wet my plants* as they asked me all sorts of questions about our bulbs. It allowed me to forget about that strange conversation with Jacob last night, or how he'd left our room before I'd even gotten out of bed.

I didn't know what time I'd finally fallen asleep, but it had felt as though the second I'd finally fallen asleep, my alarm went off. I was bleary-eyed, sleep-deprived, and had a headache waiting to stretch across my forehead and temples.

But I refused to let Jacob think what he'd said had upset me. I mean, it *had* pissed me off, but if he knew as much, he'd lord it over me. He'd say that he'd hit the nail on the head or some other stupid metaphor.

Nobody wants to be alone, sweetheart. The first and only time Jacob had called me an endearment, and he'd done it sarcastically. If that wasn't an encapsulation of the state of my love life, I didn't know what was.

Jacob also had a booth around here somewhere. He was selling seed packets from Flowers, as far as I knew. We hadn't exactly discussed the specifics. It was, however, a good reminder that our businesses were in direct competition with each other. Apparently I suffered from amnesia every time Jacob looked at me, because that important detail kept slipping from my brain.

Around lunchtime, I couldn't help but notice Jacob moving through the crowd of people, stopping at a few booths. He was catty-corner to me, getting a sample of some organic honey. This booth also featured an actual honeycomb taken from a hive that showed where they harvested the honey.

Soon, Jacob was heading my way. "How's it going?" He seemed almost...wary. Like he didn't know how I'd react if he approached me.

I might be mad at him, but I wasn't going to jump him in the middle of a convention. I was classy: I'd prefer to do it when no one else was watching.

"Well, I've sold a bunch of bulbs, I've talked about bulbs

all morning, and I'll probably be dreaming about them tonight. It'll be like the 'Dance of the Sugar Plum Fairies,' except it'll be tulip bulbs dancing."

"That sounds fucking terrifying."

I laughed. "It does. If you hear me screaming tonight, you'll know why."

At the thought of screaming in the middle of the night, my brain went to way more pleasurable reasons why that would be happening. I knew without a shadow of a doubt that Jacob was the type of man who wouldn't stop until you screamed his name in bed.

My heart started pounding, and I was glad I was sitting down, otherwise I would've gotten light-headed simply from thinking about Jacob with his head between my legs and eating my pussy with great enthusiasm.

Jacob, however, was more interested in the bulbs I was selling. "Do you dig them up in the winter?" he asked. He picked up one of the netted bags that held a single bulb.

"My dad always swore there was no reason to since we don't usually get a hard freeze, but the last few years have been so weird that I dig ours up." I went to stand next to him and pointed to the second bulb Jacob picked up, a Hawaii dahlia. "I love that kind. I planted a bunch of them a year ago and they were gorgeous in the summer."

"I like the Black Wizard." He smiled, which directed at me, made me weak in the knees. "It's my mom's favorite, too."

"Why did your parents open a store so close to ours?" I said suddenly, mostly just curious. I'd never heard the reason, despite the fact that the Wests had moved into the neighborhood over twenty years ago.

"I wish I could tell you it was because they were determined to put you guys out of business, but it was more that that's where my parents had bought a house and my mom didn't want to commute anywhere."

I stared at him. "Are you serious?"

"Totally serious." His smile grew. "My mom just hates driving in traffic."

I shook my head, chuckling. So much for my parents thinking the Wests had nefarious reasons for encroaching into our territory. Who knew it had simply been about convenience?

"I wonder what would have happened if our parents had decided to work together instead of becoming rivals?" I mused aloud.

Jacob's expression turned serious, and I was about to ask him what he was thinking about when it disappeared. "Our lives would've been way less interesting," he said finally.

"Sometimes I used to imagine what it would've been like if my parents were doctors, or accountants. Where our house wasn't filled with plants and I didn't spend summers making bouquets for weddings."

"You want to know a secret?" Jacob leaned close to me, and my breath stuttered.

"Always."

"I made the majority of the corsages we sold when I was in high school. So all those corsages at prom? I made them."

The back of my neck prickled at the mention of prom, but after his apology last night, the hurt from the incident had faded already, like a bruise turning gray.

"I'm sure the girls would've loved knowing that the most popular boy in school had made their corsages," I said.

"And I never would've heard the end of it."

"Did Tiffany know?" I blurted, because I hadn't had the courage to ask last night. "That you told me you'd go to prom with me?"

His eyes widened. "No, she didn't. She thought I wasn't going since we'd broken up."

It was a small consolation that she hadn't been in on the idea to stand me up, but it also meant the blame landed squarely on Jacob's shoulders.

He turned away and eventually chose some bulbs. I had a feeling that was going to be the end of our conversation this afternoon. *Good job, Dani.*

"I'll get these," he said as he handed me a half-dozen bulbs.

I was waiting on Jacob's credit card to process—the Wi-Fi at this place was horrendous—when the mascot for the convention, Sonny Sunflower, came lumbering past us. The costume consisted of a giant sunflower head with yellow petals that stuck out so far that pretty much every adult he walked past was smacked with a petal. A giant smiley face was in the center of the sunflower head, which was rather unsettling when leveled at you. Whoever had come up with this costume had not been thinking about basic logistics whatsoever.

Sonny waved at me and came up to my booth, only for his petal-head to hit Jacob in the face.

"Careful!" said Jacob, putting a safe distance between him and the mascot.

I started laughing so hard I felt like I was going to choke. "Sonny, you're gonna hurt somebody with those petals of yours."

Sonny put his hands up and shrugged at my declaration. Clearly, Sonny didn't care about being a public safety hazard.

"Who decided you were a good idea?" Jacob snorted. He touched one of the petals, which could bend every which way due to having a wire running through them. "You should put these in a ponytail or something. Then they wouldn't hit people."

Sonny waggled a finger, or at least, he tried to waggle a finger while wearing what basically amounted to oversized oven mitts.

"Jacob, don't molest the mascot," I chided.

Jacob kept messing with the petals. Before I knew it, he'd bent all the petals so they pointed upwards. Now Sonny looked like a sunflower that'd gotten stuck in a wind storm.

"*Jacob—*"

His grin was unrepentant. "I'm just trying to help him out."

"You're going to get us in trouble."

"What? Are they going to throw us in convention jail?"

Customers began returning from lunch, and I shooed Sonny away from my booth. I didn't have time for a giant sunflower mascot to knock over all of my bulbs because they couldn't see where they were going.

Sonny began to move through the crowd, children grabbing at his legs like barnacles. He stopped to take photos, but every time he bent down to hug a small child, a lone petal that had returned to its original position whacked the kid in the face. One started crying, causing a bit of a scene.

"It's like a train wreck," said Jacob, marveling. "I can't look away."

"Don't you have a booth to run?"

"I'm on break."

"Okay, well, don't you have someone else to bother?"

He didn't even look at me. "Nope. Just you."

One minute, I was talking to a customer about peony planting, and then I was watching what basically amounted to a slow-motion montage of a disaster. Or a train wreck, like Jacob had said.

Poor Sonny had been mobbed by children. One boy clung to Sonny's leg, and when Sonny tried to get the kid off of him, another girl pulled on Sonny's arm. Sonny lost his balance, his oversized sunflower head going straight toward the honeycomb case.

"Oh shit," said Jacob a second before Sonny hit the honeycomb.

The case exploded from the impact, the honeycomb splattering everyone in a six-foot radius. Honey hit the side of my booth and even landed on my hand. Jacob had managed to dodge most of it, although he still had a decent amount on his left pant leg.

I heard groaning, and children cried. Somebody was pushing through the crowd to help Sonny up, who was still rolling around in the honeycomb and getting stickier and stickier.

"Are you okay?" I asked, inspecting Jacob for further damage. I noticed that some honey had gotten into his hair. "You got a little here."

He grimaced, swiping at the honey, only to smear it across his forehead.

I giggled. "You're making it worse."

"You have some here." He touched my cheek, his thumb a gentle caress. After he'd wiped the honey off, he brought his thumb to his mouth and sucked it off. I suddenly couldn't breathe.

I had visions of him drizzling honey down the length of my torso before licking it off of me. As if he could read my mind, his eyes darkened.

But then somebody bumped into Jacob, effectively shattering the moment. We were back in the present, where a giant sunflower mascot was covered in honey, people were running about and yelling, and somebody announced over the intercom that there was an incident in our area and that patrons should avoid that area until it was cleaned up.

I stepped back toward my booth. "Who knew conventions could be this exciting?"

"I'm as surprised as you are," said Jacob, his gaze never leaving mine.

CHAPTER FOURTEEN

After the convention was over for the day, I returned to my room and waited for Jacob. I planned to ask him if he wanted to go to dinner with me again. My heart fluttered, thinking about what could happen *after* dinner, if I just had the balls to grab the metaphorical bull by the horns.

But time kept passing, and Jacob didn't show. Twisted up inside while so hungry, I was basically hangry at this point. I went downstairs to get some food from the hotel restaurant. I had just sat down at the bar since the restaurant was full and saw Jacob at a booth with some other people. I watched him tip his head back and laugh at something the guy next to him said.

Suddenly, my appetite disappeared. "Keep the change," I said to the bartender, bile rising in my throat. I hurried upstairs before Jacob could spot me.

I didn't understand him one bit. I wasn't stupid: he'd been flirting with me throughout this trip. He'd kissed me twice already.

First comes kissing, then comes oral, then comes fucking. Then maybe a few "I love you's" thrown in to spice things up.

Paranoid, I wondered if I'd done something to make him change his mind. Oh God, had I left a wad of hair in the bathtub drain? Had I forgotten to flush the toilet? What other disgusting things could I have done to make him decide I wasn't worth his time?

I went over every possibility, but there was only one that made sense: Jacob West was a giant douche-canoe. That was the only explanation.

It was almost 11:00 PM when Jacob came back to the room. I froze on my bed, listening to him move around in the living area. I waited for him to push the adjoining door open and say something to me. Acknowledge my existence at all. But when he didn't, I decided that I was tired of waiting for him to get his head out of his ass.

Pushing the covers off, I went into the living area without knocking. Which ended up being a bad idea that was actually an amazing idea, because he was in the middle of undressing. He'd taken off his jeans and shirt, leaving him in nothing but his boxers.

"Dani? What the—?"

"Stop talking." I wanted to enjoy this moment. It was a shame Jacob was such a douche, because he was fucking gorgeous: lean and muscular, his skin golden in the dim light. I took in his bulging arms, the angle of his elbows; I wished I could see him wearing a button-up again just for him to push the sleeves past his forearms that were way too sexy for something as benign as forearms.

His chest was heaving as I gazed at him. I moved down, down, past the patch of blond hair below his belly button, which I had the sudden urge to lick. Then to the bulge pressing against his boxers. A very noticeable, very large bulge. My stomach fluttered.

"Dani?" he repeated. His voice had gone a little hoarse.

"What the hell is your fucking deal?" I demanded. I forced myself to look only at his face. His dumb, beautiful, chiseled, haunt-you-in-your-dreams face.

"Do you want to be more specific?" His tone was wry. "Maybe when I'm wearing pants?"

"You don't get to wear pants right now." Okay, that made no sense, but I was too pissed, too aroused, too confused to care.

"I'd *love* to talk specifics. How about the fact that you flirt with me and kiss me and invite me to dinner last night, but then tonight not only do you ignore my texts, but I see you downstairs with your new friends.

"Now, I'm not saying we have to hang out every second of every day. I'm not that desperate. But you could at least not be a giant asshole with this hot-cold thing you have going on. So, yeah, I'm pissed at you. I'm pissed because you can't make up your fucking mind."

I stepped closer to him. His chest rose and fell in rapid breaths, and I wanted to laugh darkly when his gaze darted to my cleavage. Let him look—and get nothing else from me.

"You see, I'm capable of logic and reason. But you aren't, apparently. You keep doing this act like you have amnesia, Jacob. Because I'm thinking you regret ever kissing me." My voice rose on the last sentence.

Now he looked angry; red darted across his cheekbones. "I don't regret anything."

"Really? Because you're acting like you do."

"Oh, Dandelion, sweetheart." He moved until our bodies were almost aligned. "I'd love to know what you believe I'm thinking right now." He tilted his head to the side, silent. "I'm waiting."

His arrogance fed my own anger, like gasoline to a fire. "You're thinking that I'm just this weird chick obsessed with plants," I spat. "That I had a crush on you when we were kids, and gee whiz, she must still have a hard-on for me! So you tried me out, but decided I wasn't worth the trouble. Because you aren't really interested in *me*. I'm just a warm body. Any other woman would work just fine."

I was breathing hard by the end of my diatribe. Tears pricked my eyes, which only happened when I was so angry that I wanted to throw a chair. Unfortunately for me, there were no chairs light enough for me to throw at Jacob. Also I was pretty sure that, like poisoning someone, throwing chairs was illegal in Canada.

Jacob stepped toward me until our toes touched. I had to tilt my head back to see his face.

"Every single thing you said," he rumbled, "was one big, fucking lie."

I didn't realize he'd maneuvered me toward the wall until I felt my back press against it. He caged me in, just like he'd done that night under my apartment's stairs. This time, though, I wasn't drunk, and I could see every emotion flash across his face. I could make out the dark blond stubble on his jaw, a little nick near his ear he must've made this morning while shaving.

In that moment, I felt trapped, desired, angry, confused. I didn't know if I wanted to pull him closer or jam my fist into his solar plexus.

"Why do I feel like you're full of shit?" I shot back. "You keep saying one thing and doing another."

"You're right." My eyes widened at his confession. He pushed a strand of my hair behind my ear. "But that's the only thing you're right about."

"I don't believe you."

His blue eyes flashed. I'd never been afraid of Jacob, but I was afraid of him for a split second. Not that he'd hurt me—no, he'd never hurt me. Not physically. But I was afraid because I knew how easily he could break my heart, the heart that I'd tried to protect for so long.

"I never thought of you as some 'weird plant girl,' for one. It would be a bit hypocritical for me to think that, anyway."

I looked away, annoyed.

"And I haven't been *trying you out*." He sounded so disgusted that I turned back to look at him. Anger filled his face, his voice. "If you think, for one damn second, that I haven't wanted you with every fiber of my being since the first moment I saw you in your store, you're wrong. I told myself to leave you well enough alone, but I'm not a saint, Dani."

My chin trembled. "I never asked you to be a saint."

"Good, because tonight isn't about sainthood." He grasped my chin. "The last thing on my mind is being good. I want to do bad things to you. Until the only thing you can say is, 'more, Jacob.' Until I'm buried so deep inside you that you can't breathe. Until your tight little pussy squeezes around my cock when you come."

I definitely couldn't breathe now. I could feel his cock, hard as iron, against my belly. My panties were already soaked. If he touched me, he'd feel how much I wanted him, no matter what I tried to tell myself otherwise.

He kissed me—finally. It wasn't just a kiss, though: it was like being consumed. Tipping my head back, he stroked my jaw, urging me to open my mouth. And I did. I surrendered to him, like our fight had never happened. His tongue brushed mine, and I reciprocated.

He groaned, pressing me harder against the wall, fucking my mouth like I'd imagined he'd fuck my pussy. I couldn't stop shivering. My nipples were hardened to diamond points. Between every kiss I gasped for breath, but I didn't care if I stopped breathing. I never wanted Jacob to stop kissing me.

"Tell me you want this," he said, hoarse now. He brushed his thumb over my bottom lip. "Tell me, or I'll never touch you again." Even as he said the words, he leaned down to kiss the shell of my ear.

"Tell me. Tell me to leave you alone." He sounded almost like he wanted me to say those very words.

But my body had taken over my mind. I was a bundle of need, desire, desperation. Yet instead of saying something sexy like, "Take me, I'm yours," I blurted, "I'm a virgin."

I'd played this scenario out in my head so many times already. When I told Jacob I was a virgin, he would either look horrified and run in the opposite direction, screaming; or, he'd laugh at me, because I was obviously joking.

To my astonishment, he didn't laugh. He didn't scream. He didn't say anything. He just pushed the strap of my tank top down my arm to kiss my shoulder.

"I wondered," he murmured. His tongue was a heated stroke against my skin.

"You mean you *knew?*"

"You did say that night in your apartment you hadn't had guys over." He almost looked apologetic, like he'd read my diary. "I didn't think you were a virgin, but just—inexperienced."

I blushed. I didn't know if it was from nerves or from the fact that Jacob hadn't pushed me away. I hadn't realized how anxious I'd been to tell him that I was a virgin.

"I was afraid you'd judge me," I whispered. I buried my face in his shoulder.

"Dani, look at me." I forced myself to obey him. "I don't care if you're a virgin, or if you've fucked a million guys."

My eyes widened. "A million would be pretty impressive."

"It would, but that's not the point." He kissed my forehead, then my nose. His lips were whisper soft. "Your self-worth isn't based on who you have or haven't screwed."

Tears of relief pricked my eyes. "Really?"

"Really. We'll take this as slow or as fast as you want. You're in control. If you don't like anything, you'll tell me, okay?"

I perked up. "Is this like *Fifty Shades of Grey*? Should we come up with a safe word?"

"Sorry to disappoint you, but I don't have a room full of whips and chains."

I stuck out my bottom lip. "How boring of you."

"Dani, I run a flower shop. How could I afford an entire room for chaining up women?"

That was a fair point. "But I thought all Seattle guys had a red room?" I tried to sound innocent.

"Choose a safe word." He began to kiss me behind my ear, the spot especially sensitive. My brain seemed to forget what words even were. How could I choose *one?* I didn't know any, except Jacob. And that wouldn't really work as a safe word.

"Hyacinth," I squeaked as Jacob cupped my breast. "Nobody says that during sex."

"Apparently you've never had sex in a garden," he quipped.

Feeling bold all of a sudden, I pressed my hand over his heart, which was beating like a drum. I ran my fingers across his pectorals, enjoying the crisp texture of hair over the firm muscles. I brushed one of his nipples, and he hissed out a breath.

As I moved downward toward his cock, still hard and outlined by his thin boxers, my pussy clenched with need. I might've not known the ins and outs of sex, but my body knew what it wanted. And what it wanted was Jacob West.

He kissed me again before lifting me up into his arms and carrying me to my bed. After he'd set me down, never breaking our kiss, he pushed the other strap of my tank top down my arm. My tank was loose and I never wore a bra to bed. When the fabric fell below my breasts, my nipples now exposed to the cool air, his pupils dilated.

"I take back what I said," he muttered. "I should be the only man to see these tits of yours."

I shuddered, and I shuddered again when he licked around one peak. He pushed me back onto the bed, my legs widening instinctively to allow him room. He sucked my nipples until they ached. I kept arching against him, needing more contact. I was a live wire about to explode.

"I've wanted to know if your nipples are as pink as your pussy." Jacob kissed down my torso and then very slowly pushed my sleep shorts down, revealing my cotton panties. When I sucked in a breath, he said, "You okay?"

"Yes," I squeaked.

"Because you looked terrified right then."

"I am, but that doesn't mean I want you to stop."

He looked dubious. To prove I wasn't just appeasing him, I took off my panties, completely naked now. I was blushing all over. No man had seen me completely naked before, and it was—exhilarating. Nobody had looked at me like Jacob looked at me right now.

"Spread your legs," he instructed.

My thighs quivered as I lay back down. I hadn't yet exposed myself to him. I suddenly wished we'd turned out the lights. What if he didn't like what he saw?

"You're thinking too much," he said.

"How can you tell?"

He smiled. "I told you. You narrow your eyes when you're thinking." He murmured reassurances, dirty words. He kissed my knees, licked at my ankles.

Finally I found the courage to spread my legs, my pussy on display. I was already soaking. I covered my eyes, because it was too much to watch him.

"Don't." His voice was guttural. "I want you to watch this."

I couldn't breathe. I watched as he lightly petted the soft curls covering my mound. I was afraid I'd come before he'd even begun touching me.

He parted my pussy lips, groaning deep in his throat as he slicked a finger through the folds. "I was right," he said, "your pussy is just as pink as your nipples."

"Oh my God."

Every feeling, every sensation, centered right where Jacob touched me. He caressed me, avoiding my clit, despite my best attempts to buck into his hand. He strummed my body like a string instrument. Wetness seeped from my body, and if I weren't so wild for release, I would've died of embarrassment.

"Tell me what you like," he said. His index finger danced around my throbbing clit.

"Harder," I gasped.

He lightly brushed my clit, like a butterfly wing of a caress. When I arched, wanting more, he increased the pressure. I moaned. "Wait, wait. A little bit more—yes."

"You're so gorgeous, Dani, your pussy wet and aching for me." He continued to circle my clit, tapping it a few times, which made my toes curl into the bedspread.

He didn't stop playing with my clit as he slowly pressed a finger inside my channel. I jerked in surprise, even his single index finger feeling like an invasion.

He swore under his breath. "Fuck, you're tight. I can barely get one finger inside you."

I quivered. My heart was pounding in my ears. Jacob petted my leg, soothing me, and soon I was begging for more. More, more, more. It was the only word I knew right then.

"I want you to come for me," he said, finger-fucking me as he rubbed my clit. "I can feel you gripping my finger. Jesus, Dani."

My vision blurred. I couldn't speak. I could only moan, and beg, and writhe as he made my body do exactly what he wanted it to do. I was a slave to his mastery. Tears leaked from my eyes. My release drew closer and closer, the orgasm just out of reach.

"Jacob," I cried out.

"I got you, sweetheart. Let go. I'll catch you."

I did. I let go—I fell off the cliff, my cry filling the room. I shook, Jacob continuing to draw out my release with his brilliant, magical fingers.

He wrapped me in his arms afterward, and I realized I needed to hold onto something after what had just happened. It wasn't just my body that had flown apart: it was my heart. I'd thought it had been so well protected. I'd thought—I didn't know anymore.

I buried my face in Jacob's shoulder like before as he kissed me.

"Can I ask you a question?" I said, gulping in air still.

"Sure."

"Since you've basically half-deflowered me, can I have your phone number finally?"

CHAPTER FIFTEEN

I fell in love with Jacob a third time when I was seventeen. I also fell *out* of love with him at seventeen.

Yes, this is the prom story.

In April of my senior year of high school, Anna came skipping up to me at lunch, her face flushed. She proceeded to tell me that Sam from band had asked her to prom, despite our pact that we wouldn't attend because prom was dumb.

"You know it's going to be too many people packed into the Country Lodge, with the deer heads on the walls, and everyone's going to be drunk and sweaty," I said. "And Sam is probably going to try to grope you in the back of his pickup afterward. Wow, sounds fun."

"Now you're just being a jerk." Anna grabbed her lunch and stood up. "And Sam doesn't drive a pickup. He drives his mom's minivan."

With that parting shot, Anna left me to sit at lunch alone. She was always my lunch buddy—my only one. If either of us was sick, the days were long and lonely without each other.

Guilt sat in my stomach like lead. I was about to go after Anna when the bell rang. I'd have to apologize after school.

As I walked to physics, I watched Jacob with his group of friends. I thought of when he'd acted like he'd given me that valentine back in eighth grade when any other boy would've told me to get lost. I thought of what it would be like to go to prom with Jacob West.

What if I asked him, and he said yes?

My fight with Anna continued as the days passed, mostly because Anna refused to talk to me. I texted her over and over, until finally, she simply replied, *stop texting me.*

If Anna was going to prom with her date, then I was going to have one, too. By Thursday, I'd managed to get up enough courage to ask Jacob myself. I'd rehearsed the words I would say in the mirror at home. Before lunch, I went into the girl's bathroom and rehearsed for the last time. Until a girl yelled at me through a stall door to shut up because she couldn't pee with me talking to myself.

I waited until school ended. I knew Jacob often hung out in the atrium with his friends until they had practice. If I were lucky, I could catch him before he went to track practice.

When I found him sitting on a bench by himself, messing with his phone, I considered it a sign from the universe. From God himself, Buddha, the Flying Spaghetti Monster—all three combined were shining down on me and saying, *Jacob is yours. Ask and ye shall receive a date to prom.*

"Hi," I said.

Jacob didn't look up from his phone.

"Hi," I said more loudly.

Finally, he heard me. "Hi," he said. He sounded confused. I couldn't blame him: we rarely talked anymore. Sometimes we'd walk past each other going home, but beyond a few "hey's" and "bye's," we weren't exactly best friends. Jacob hadn't even asked for my notes since we'd started high school. We didn't have many classes that overlapped.

"I wanted to ask you something." The words tumbled from mouth, so quickly that it sounded more like *Iwanttoaskyou-something.* Before Jacob could say no, I added, "Do you want to go to prom with me?"

A faint blush climbed up his cheeks. His phone chimed, but he didn't look at it. He was just looking at me, like I was some new species he'd discovered.

Then, he said the words I'd only ever daydreamed hearing: "Okay."

My face was so red at this point that I was sure I was on fire. "Really?"

"Yeah. Sure."

It wasn't exactly the effusive reaction I'd wanted, but it was enough. My heart practically burst inside me with excitement.

I'm going to prom with Jacob. He said yes. I'm going to prom with JACOB WEST.

"YOU LOOK BEAUTIFUL, DANDELION." My dad finished one last tweak on my corsage and placed it on my wrist. It was made up of white roses and violets, the flowers' meanings not lost on me at all.

"Did you seriously give me a corsage with flowers that mean purity and modesty?" I groused. "What do you think we're going to be doing at prom?"

Dad cleared his throat. "It's more to warn him off. If he knows anything about flowers—which he *should*—he'll know you aren't a girl who gets around."

"*Dad.*"

"So when is this boy coming?" He said the words *this boy* like you would say *this rabid raccoon.* My parents had never come around to Jacob West, but when I'd told them in no uncertain terms that he was taking me to prom and they could either like it or not, they decided to keep their mouths shut for once.

"He said he'd be here by five o'clock."

My palms were sweaty with anticipation. I was glad I'd put on extra deodorant because I was so nervous that I was sure to pit out my dress. When I'd told Anna that Jacob had agreed to go to prom with me, she'd been so surprised that she'd broken her silent treatment with me. We'd found dresses together— her, a red strapless number, me, a green puffy silk dress that looked like something out of my garden—but we decided to meet at the restaurant together before going over to the Country Lounge.

"Oh, you look so beautiful." My mom wiped a tear from her eye. "Kate, stop tearing apart that doll and tell your sister she's pretty."

Kate glanced up at me and shrugged. "Her hair is too big."

"And your nose is too big," I said. Kate just stuck out her tongue and returned to whatever evil experiment she was doing on her Barbie. I'd stopped asking her what she was doing years ago. I figured it was safer for all of us. I almost wished Mari was here, but she was attending college down at Oregon State.

My parents took pictures of me, making me stand by my dad's orchids and even holding one of his favorites, a Dossinia jewel orchid, with its deep burgundy leaves laced with pink, green and gold that sparkled in the light. I'm pretty sure he loved that plant more than me and my sisters combined, but he also said it needed way more care than we did, so I couldn't be offended that he loved a plant more than me. My mom then had me go outside and take more photos with her rosebushes. Finally, I told them my feet hurt and I returned inside to wait for Jacob.

It was four-thirty. I'd told him that I was wearing green, so I assumed he'd wear a matching green tie. Jacob would look amazing in a tux, I thought. I could see it now: him ringing the doorbell, a bouquet in his hand. I'd answer it, and he'd stare at me in shock before stuttering out how beautiful I was.

And maybe if I were really, really lucky, he'd kiss me in the car before he dropped me off at home.

Kate kept me company as I waited. At ten, she was pretty much a baby genius with an aptitude for taking things apart and putting them back together again. The only reason she still wanted dolls was because she liked to rearrange their limbs, so they had legs for arms and vice versa. She often figured out a way to take off their painted faces, or cut their hair until they were bald.

By the time it was five o'clock, I sat on the edge of the couch, all anticipation. The minutes ticked by. I checked my phone: 5:10, 5:17. By 5:25, I thought about texting Jacob, but I didn't want to seem like I was bugging him. He was probably just getting ready still. We weren't meeting Anna and Sam at the restaurant until six-thirty, anyway.

By 5:45, I was pacing the living room. My parents had

both popped in to ask where Jacob was, my dad frowning deeply at Jacob's lack of punctuality.

"He'll be here," I kept saying. Mostly because I had to believe it for myself. I texted him, but no response. I texted him again, but silence. I felt nauseous. Had something happened to him? Worry knotted my gut.

Finally tired of waiting, I decided to go to his house. Not caring that I was teetering in high heels, I walked to his house —all of three houses down—my brain imagining all kinds of terrible scenarios.

That was when I saw Jacob walking out of his house with Tiffany, his supposed ex-girlfriend. I hid behind one of the tall hedges that stood in front of his house.

I watched as Jacob opened the passenger door for Tiffany before climbing into the driver's seat. Neither of them were wearing prom clothes. And in a blink, they drove away.

It didn't take a rocket scientist to figure out what had just happened. After I got home and locked my bedroom door, I took out the dandelion wreath and the valentine I'd kept for so many years, hidden in a shoebox under my bed, and I tore them all up.

And thus my love for Jacob died a swift death on that night almost a decade ago.

CHAPTER SIXTEEN

Kate snapped her fingers in front of my face. "Dani, are you even listening to me?"

The answer to that was definitely *no*, but I lied and said, "Yes."

Kate snorted. "You know those hearts that float above anime characters' heads when they're in love? That's what you looked like. Plus some major heart eyes. I'd throw up but I paid six dollars for this latte and that would be a waste of perfectly good coffee."

After my *encounter* with Jacob, things had...shifted. Good shifted. Since we'd both come back to Seattle—and he'd given me his phone number after laughing at me for at least five minutes—we'd been texting each other nonstop. The only reason we hadn't continued our sex escapade was because I'd had to create a bunch of arrangements at the last minute for an elopement, and Jacob had had all kinds of work-related things pop up, although he never alluded to what, exactly, they were.

"I wasn't making heart eyes," I said, wrinkling my nose. "I was just thinking."

"Thinking about your one true love, Jacob?" At my surprise, Kate laughed. "I saw your phone when you went to the bathroom." She wiggled her eyebrows. "Getting hot and heavy, huh?"

"Oh my God." I groaned, putting my head in my hands. I did not need my younger sister razzing me. Not to mention I was pretty sure she was a virgin, too, so it wasn't like she could act like she knew more than me on that front.

"Hey, no judgment. I've always thought this whole rivalry was dumb. Plus, he's hot. I saw him come out of their store and I was like, 'Damn, Dani. Get that ass.'"

"Please stop talking."

"I'm not the one getting dick pics at a coffee shop."

Jacob had sent me a dick pic? Frantic, I looked at my phone, only to find a fairly benign text waiting for me. *Red roses or pink?*

"You little shit," I grumbled as Kate laughed like a maniacal cartoon villain. "Jacob would never send me a dick pic, anyway." Although even as I said the words, I was kind of disappointed, thinking that he wouldn't. Even though I hadn't gotten to look at his cock except what I had seen through his boxers, I knew he was packing.

My pussy tingled. Memories flooded my brain, and along with them, memories of every sensation Jacob had stroked and rubbed out of me. I squeezed my thighs together and willed my body to calm down. Lately it was like a stiff breeze could set me off like some horny weirdo.

"Like I said," said Kate, "heart eyes."

"Did you ask me to coffee just to make fun of me?

Because I'd rather pick snails out of the vegetable garden than sit through this."

Kate dipped her chin down, making her seem deceptively young and innocent. Well, she *was* young, but she wasn't innocent. She'd been born evil, in the way that younger sisters were born to torment you. She had a sweet, heart-shaped face, her chin a bit pointy but endearing, nonetheless. With her wide brown eyes and long lashes, she could make puppy eyes with the best of them.

Kate dressed like she'd rifled through a dumpster for her clothes, which tended to mask how pretty she was: oversized sweatshirts with various logos on them, torn-up jeans, and sneakers way past their expiration date consisted of her usual outfit. In the summer, she just swapped the jeans for jean shorts. She never left her hair down, but instead, either braided it or put it in a topknot at the crown of her head.

The last time I'd seen her wear a dress had been when she was seven and had been a flower girl in a family friend's wedding. She'd taken off the dress and put on jeans within five minutes of the wedding ending, to my mom's dismay.

"Spill it," I said, pointing my coffee stirrer at her. "What did you do?"

She widened her eyes further. "Me? Do something? I am innocent as a lamb, guiltless as Jesus Christ himself—"

"And as full of shit as a bag of fertilizer."

"You would use fertilizer in a metaphor."

I raised an eyebrow and waited.

Kate played with a straw wrapper, fidgeting in her chair. "Well, there's this boy," she hedged.

"A boy you like?"

A blush climbed up her cheeks. "Maybe."

131

I had no idea why she'd wanted to talk to me about boy problems instead of Mari, but I was too intrigued to tell her as much. I couldn't remember Kate *ever* liking a boy. She'd always been one of the boys, in fact. I had a feeling those boys had lumped her in with them and Kate had never cared to change their opinions.

"He's in my chemistry class. He's my lab partner, actually. We were in the same dorm freshman year, but then, when everyone moved into apartments, I didn't see him. Until this class."

"What's his name?"

She put her hands over her red cheeks. "Grayson."

"Do you think he likes you, too?"

"I don't know. That's the thing. He's nice to me, but he had a girlfriend up until a month ago. She was the complete opposite of me." Kate waved a hand down her body. "She wore pink and lip gloss. She carried a tote instead of a backpack. You know, *those* girls."

"Nothing wrong with wearing pink," I pointed out.

Now Kate looked annoyed. "Well, duh. It's just that boys tend to like girls who are…girls." She tucked a strand of hair behind her ear. "But I don't know how to do that, you know?"

"Not that I mind talking to you about this, but this seems like a conversation for Mari, not me. I'm not exactly glamorous."

"Mari is too caught up in her wedding, and then she'd want to give me a makeover as she talked about how David said this or did that." Kate wrinkled her nose. "Last time I talked to Mari, she kept going on and on about how David finally decided to get a haircut even though his favorite barber retired so he had to find a new one. Apparently, it was a huge deal."

My lips twitched. "Fair point."

"Besides, you've been looking really pretty lately."

I hadn't thought anyone had noticed that I'd started wearing makeup and doing something with my standard brown hair beyond pulling it back in a ponytail. "Oh, thanks."

"You're welcome." Kate paused. "So, what should I do?"

I considered my answer, not wanting to give Kate bad advice. "I'm not exactly the best person to ask, you know. I'm not good at talking about how I feel. The last time I put myself out there for a guy, he stood me up for prom."

Kate winced. "Yeah, he was a shithead for that. Did he ever say why?"

"He did, but I'll tell you about that later." I tapped my chin. "I think what you need to do is see if you can hang out with Grayson outside of school. See how he acts around you. Maybe do it in a group first, then go from there."

"Like ask him out on a date?"

"It is the twenty-first century. That's allowed."

Kate snorted. "Do you think I care about some stupid sexist convention?" She sighed. "It sounds terrifying. What if he says no?"

"Then you'll have your answer, at least."

"Should I put on mascara? Wear pink?" She wrinkled her nose. "No, that's going way too far."

"Katie-cat, if he doesn't like you for you, then changing yourself isn't going to make a difference. That being said, maybe you *want* to wear some makeup. Ever thought about that?"

"Maybe," she grudgingly replied. "Will you help me?" she

whispered, and if we weren't in a crowded coffee shop, I would've hugged her and totally embarrassed her.

As I walked home and Kate returned to her apartment on campus, I knew that I'd given her good advice, but I still felt like a hypocrite. When I'd been in her shoes, I always kept my feelings to myself because I assumed a boy like that wouldn't be interested in me. Even though I demanded honesty in people, I realized that I hadn't demanded it of myself, because I'd told myself that me not saying anything wouldn't hurt anyone.

Except, it had hurt me, in a subtler way. If I didn't put myself out there, then I couldn't get hurt, right? I'd held myself back in terms of relationships for a long time. Anna probably had a point: I did tend to pick the guys I subconsciously knew wouldn't work out for me, which meant there was no risk.

This whole thing with Jacob scared the bejeezus out of me. Part of me wanted to scuttle away and act like he'd never awakened this *need* inside of me—not just sexual, but that was a part of it. Feelings I'd long since repressed had surfaced with a speed that gave me whiplash.

But how could I tell my little sister to be brave if I couldn't be brave, too?

I had just made up my mind when I walked past a French cafe that had amazing macarons. I stopped for a second, wondering if I should give in and buy some (the owner knew my name and my favorite flavors at this point), when I saw a familiar golden head at a table in the corner. And sitting across from Jacob was Tiffany McClain, her smile wide and beautiful.

All that stuff I'd thought about her when she'd treated

Kevin—that I'd forgiven her, that she was different—was a lie. A big, smelly lie. I hated her in that moment and I hated Jacob, too, and I knew that I'd convicted them both without a trial and I didn't care.

My stomach curdled. The thought of macarons made me want to die, which was probably the saddest thing ever. What did macarons do to get lumped in with this icky, viscous feeling of betrayal? Nothing.

You don't know anything's happening, I told myself.

I told myself that, except that evil little voice in my brain reminded me that Tiffany had been Jacob's first love, and he'd stood me up for prom when she'd decided she'd wanted him back. What if this was just Part Two?

I imagined going inside the cafe, buying a bunch of macarons, and pelting them at the gorgeous duo. It only made me feel marginally better.

Jacob turned his head, and his gaze met mine. His eyes widened. I totally panicked, and I started running.

Another thing I never do: run. Running is terrible. It was invented by Satan and pushed by people who hated themselves. To quote the best TV show of our time, *Parks and Recreation,* "Jogging is the worst. I mean, I know it keeps you healthy, but God, at what cost?"

I didn't get far before I heard Jacob yelling, "Dani! Stop!"

He caught up with me within five seconds, damn him and his long legs. At this point I was wheezing like someone who smoked five packs a day. My breasts hurt. Running was not meant to happen when you had boobs bouncing around like I did.

"Are you okay?" Jacob tried to take my arm, but I wouldn't let him.

"I'm." Wheeze. "Fine." Wheeze. "Go." Wheeze. "Away." Wheeze.

"You look like you're going to faint. Here, sit down."

I was too winded to resist him. I sat on a bench and, somehow, I found my head between my knees. I wondered if I would make this worse and puke all over Jacob's shoes again. That would certainly add a nice cherry on top to this shit sundae.

Once I finally caught my breath and the redness in my face had receded, I said, "What was that all about?"

Jacob didn't even flinch. He didn't look guilty, even though he should feel very, very guilty. Except—we hadn't said we were exclusive, had we? Oh God, why had I thought that? I should've known this was all too good to be true.

Panic spiraled through me. The logical part of my brain kept telling me to calm down, but that part kept getting smaller. It was like a tiny pebble trying to stop an ocean wave from pulling it out to sea.

"Why were you with Tiffany McClain?"

"Would you believe me if I told you the reason?"

I just glared at him, crossing my arms across my chest.

"You were having dinner with her, and you looked like you were on a date. She had heart eyes," I accused.

Jacob's lips twitched. "Heart eyes? Really?"

"Yes. I would know." *Because I always have them around you.* "Her body language screamed, DO ME, JACOB."

"You got all that from, what, ten seconds?"

I sighed, hanging my head over the bench. "I know all about looking at somebody you want," I said vaguely. "Believe me."

Jacob didn't say anything for a long moment, and I waited

for the inevitable blow. *We aren't exclusive. I never said I liked you. It was just a one-time thing. Tiffany wants to try again and I still love her.*

"If Tiffany was looking at me with heart eyes," said Jacob finally, "then it would be pretty weird that she wanted to talk to me about a special arrangement for when she proposes to her girlfriend this weekend."

I was glad I was sitting down, because my world tilted on its axis right then. It took me a second to understand what Jacob had said, but when it clicked in my brain, I could only say, "Ooooooh."

Jacob smiled. "Yeah, pretty much."

"I didn't know she was gay. Or bi, since she dated you. Not that it's my business." I cleared my throat. "Well, I feel stupid."

Jacob just raised an eyebrow.

"Really stupid?"

"How about supremely stupid?" he said.

I scowled. "Okay, I jumped to a dumb conclusion, but can you blame me? You guys have a history, and she's..." I trailed off, looking away.

Jacob touched my chin, forcing me to look at him again. "Dani, do you really think, after what happened between us, I'd dump you and go straight back to my high school ex-girlfriend, who I haven't thought about in years, by the way?"

I squirmed. "I'm sorry."

He stroked my jaw, and I leaned into his touch like a cat. I could feel a purr almost rumbling in my throat as he touched my ear, my cheek. "We were over a long time ago. And as far as I can tell, she's in love with her girlfriend. She couldn't stop talking about her."

"When did they start dating?" I said.

"I didn't ask." His tone was wry.

"Only because…" And here I started smiling like a crazy person. "I wonder if you were the one who made her decide to join the other team."

Now it was Jacob's turn to scowl. "If we weren't in public, I'd turn you over my knee for that comment."

I shivered. Feeling bold, I kissed him and said, "I'd like to see you try."

"Oh, I plan to try lots of things with you." He pulled my hair—gently—tilting my head back. "I'm coming over Friday night."

"Are you asking or telling?"

"Telling. Also, don't wear any nice underwear."

I swallowed, my throat dry. "Why not?"

"Because I'm going to shred it otherwise." He kissed me, hard, then said, "I have to get back to Tiffany. She couldn't decide if she wanted freesia or violets."

"You're so hot when you talk flowers."

After he stood up, he leaned down to whisper in my ear, "I'll be even hotter when I'm inside you. Now go home before I make good and spank you right here on this bench, sweetheart."

CHAPTER SEVENTEEN

When I opened the door to my apartment Friday night, I expected Jacob.

What I didn't expect was Jacob wearing a tuxedo and with a corsage in his hand, a boutonniere pinned to his lapel.

His expression serious, although I could see a smile at the edges of his mouth, he said, "Are you ready for prom?"

I glanced down at my outfit: jean shorts and a V-neck shirt. At least I'd put on some makeup. "I don't exactly have a prom dress hanging out in my closet," I said. I'd gotten rid of the one I'd planned to wear the next day after Jacob had stood me up.

Jacob stepped into my apartment. "That's fine. We can have prom here."

He handed me the bouquet—an arrangement of pink roses and sunflowers—and then said, "Put out your hand."

He put the corsage on my wrist. This one also had pink roses. "Did you make this?"

"I did. Do you like it?"

"I love it." My heart felt like it was going to spill over. "I can't believe you did this."

"It's nine years late, but I thought I'd make it up to you. I thought I'd tell you to dress up, but I didn't want to ruin the surprise."

"Oh, believe me, I'm not disappointed that I didn't have to squish myself into a bunch of Spanx."

His gaze was heated as he looked at my breasts, cleavage visible above the rather plunging V-neck. "That would be a travesty." He reached behind me and squeezed my ass. "None of this should be hidden."

"You're an ass man?"

"Baby, I'm an anything man. And you have so much to enjoy."

His kiss was long, reminding me that, despite the corsage and talk of prom, we weren't awkward teenagers anymore. And Jacob knew what he was doing, but that didn't help my nerves that much. I'd been on edge all day, waiting for the evening to come—pun intended. What if I messed everything up? What if Jacob was disappointed in me?

"You're thinking again," he said. He traced a line down the middle of my forehead.

"Sorry. It's a habit of mine."

"What are you thinking about?"

"Oh, you know. The usual. If this is going to be any good. If *I'm* going to be any good. If I'm going to fuck it all up."

"It's going to be good. Wasn't it already good?"

I smiled, blushing at the memory. "More than good. Amazing."

"And we haven't even gotten to the main event yet." He

kissed the side of my neck. "But we aren't going to rush things, either."

I quivered as he licked a path down my throat. "Wait, why not?" Suddenly I wanted to rush things very, very badly.

"Because you're not just going to lose your virginity to me, Dani. I'm going to ruin you for any other man."

Well, shit, I thought rather wildly. *I totally believe him, too.*

He led me to the living room, and after messing with his phone, he started playing music straight from our senior year in high school. Kevin sat on top of his cat tree like a grumpy chaperon, his tail swishing when Jacob got too close.

"Your cat isn't going to kill me, is he?" said Jacob as Taylor Swift's "You Belong With Me" started playing.

"Just don't make eye contact with him."

"Duly noted."

We started slow dancing, Jacob's hands on my waist, and when he attempted to twirl me in a circle and we got all tangled up, we both started laughing.

"Since we're not seventeen, I think we need some drinks." I went to my fridge, glad that I'd stocked up on wine and beer. "Want anything?"

"I'll have a beer."

I poured myself a glass of Pinot Grigio and brought Jacob a beer.

"Who bought you the booze?" said Jacob, like we were still actually teenagers. "I had a guy but he moved to San Diego and now I've been up shit creek without a paddle."

I sniffed. "A lady never discloses where she acquires illicit booze."

He snorted and drank his beer. I couldn't but be enthralled by his Adam's apple bobbing, the way his throat worked. With the last remaining rays of sunlight filtering through my blinds, he seemed mysterious, alluring. It helped that the heat in his gaze was liable to set me on fire at any moment.

Another slow song, "Just the Way You Are" by Bruno Mars, began playing. Jacob took my glass of wine and his beer and set them on the coffee table. He put his hands back on my waist, but soon those hands drifted further down.

I widened my eyes. "Jacob——" I mock-gasped. I took his hands, moved them back up. "Behave yourself. There are chaperons watching." I pointed to Kevin, who had just fallen asleep. His eye opened for a second before he fell back asleep. So much for being chaperoned.

"You're right." Instead of keeping his hands on my waist, he moved them up until they cupped both of my breasts. I inhaled a sharp breath. "Is this too high?" he asked innocently.

"Yes," I squeaked, mostly because he just brushed both of my nipples.

"You don't sound convinced."

I moaned as he pinched one swollen peak and rolled the other between his fingertips. "Jacob——"

In a quick movement, he pressed me tightly against him. I could feel his hardness against my belly, and the thought that I'd feel that inside me made me almost melt at his feet. I wanted everything he could give me. I didn't care if it hurt—it would be worth it.

He grabbed my ass again before spanking one cheek. I yelped in surprise. "That was for the other day." He spanked the other cheek. The pain somehow translated to pleasure, and I almost wanted to beg him to keep spanking me.

"Oh no." I fluttered my eyelashes. "Have I been a bad girl?" My voice was breathy.

His pupils dilated. Groaning, he grabbed my hair and kissed me like a wild man. His tongue plunged into my mouth, the kiss hot and wet. It was messy and desperate, and I loved it. I ran my fingers through the hair at the nape of his neck, enjoying the strands' silky softness.

"Tell me you want this," he said. He sounded like he was about to fall off the edge. "Because I won't be able to stop."

Words felt inadequate in that moment. I stepped away from him and took off my t-shirt. Despite his admonition not to wear sexy underwear, I hadn't listened. What woman was going to lose her virginity wearing granny panties and a sports bra if she could avoid it? I'd recently splurged on an emerald green lace bra and thong set that I had hoped Jacob would get to see, but it wasn't until this moment that I believed it.

Jacob's eyes were darker than I'd ever seen them. "Keep going." His voice was like velvet and steel.

My hands shook, but not from fear: from anticipation. I slipped off my cat socks, laughing a little at how incongruous they were with what was happening, before my jean shorts went straight to the floor.

Jacob drank me in. My nipples hardened, my pussy flooding with moisture simply from him gazing at me. I'd never thought a man could look at me like he wanted to ravish me on the spot, but then again, I'd never thought any of this would be happening in the first place.

"Should I keep going?" I said, reaching around to take off my bra.

"No." Jacob moved, staying my hand. "Not yet." He cleared his throat. "We should talk about protection."

I had to bite back a smile at his serious tone. "Yes, that would be the responsible thing to do."

"I brought condoms. I assumed you didn't have any."

"You assumed correctly. Besides, I would've chosen the wrong size or type. It'd kind of be like you buying me tampons without my specifying which type."

Jacob looked like he was going to cry with laughter, which only made me want to laugh, too.

"In case you were wondering," he continued, "I'm clean."

I swallowed, my mouth going dry. I didn't know what devil decided to perk up on my shoulder, but I found myself saying, "I'm on birth control already because I'm vain about my skin. Which is rather convenient, I know. So we can skip the condoms. If you want."

A predatory smile stretched across his face. He kissed my shoulder and murmured in my ear, "Good, because I really wanted to go bare inside you, but didn't know if you'd be cool with it."

"I'm cool. Super cool. The absolute coolest. Coolio cool."

He nipped my collarbone. "You're adorable."

He kept kissing and nipping and licking, which meant he was already taking control again. Before he could turn me into a puddle at his feet, I said, "Take off your jacket. And then roll the sleeves up."

"You're giving orders now?" But he smiled and did as I asked. His tossed his jacket and tie onto the couch, almost hitting Kevin, who'd moved from his perch on top of the cat tree. Hissing, Kevin slinked off into my room with a look of betrayal.

"He's probably never going to forgive me," I said mournfully.

"He'll get over it." Jacob rolled up his shirtsleeves and revealed the tanned length of his forearms covered in light golden hair. "Turn around and put your hands on the wall."

My belly quivered. For a long moment, I stared at the wall, waiting for him to touch me. To do anything to me. Finally, he cupped my bare ass, only a strip of the thong covering it now. He pushed the strap aside and stroked my pussy, swearing when he felt how wet I was already.

He kissed the side of my neck as he played with me. His touch was gentle, almost soothing, but it only made things worse because I wanted hard and rough and fast. I wanted more, more, more, but Jacob just held me against the wall, his body solid and unmovable, as he stroked me.

"That night in the hotel room," he said, his breath hot on my neck, "it took everything I had not to eat your pussy until my mouth was drenched in you."

"Why didn't you?" I gasped when he tapped my clit.

"Because I knew that once I ate your pussy, I wouldn't stop there." He circled my sheath before pressing two fingers inside me. I reflexively bucked against his hand, like I wanted him to stop.

"Am I hurting you?"

"No. I mean, yes, but it's a good hurt." The initial burn had faded, and I just wanted him to plunge his fingers inside me until I contracted around him.

"A good hurt?" He swiped across my clit as he finger-fucked me like he had in the hotel room. "What if I add a third one? Can you take it, sweetheart?"

I whimpered. When he added a third, stars burst across my vision. I was already so full. How could I take his cock, which I knew was thicker than even three of his fingers?

He pulled his fingers out before thrusting back inside, his thumb massaging my clit at the same time. Moisture dripped from my pussy. I couldn't speak—I couldn't think. I was so close to orgasm that I could only beg like a crazy woman.

But right when I was about to come, he stopped. I protested on a groan.

"I want you to come with my mouth on your pussy," he said before he went down on his knees. In short measure, he pulled my thong to my ankles, widened my legs, and maneuvered me so I was bent at almost a ninety-degree angle.

I was completely exposed. I was glad he couldn't see my face, because my cheeks were burning. But any embarrassment faded away when he licked through my swollen folds.

I cried out. "Jacob—" I wished I had something to hold onto.

"Fuck, you're sweet. You taste amazing." His growl reverberated through my entire body.

As he ate me out, I felt my orgasm once again coalescing, deep in my belly. My palms were sweaty. My nipples hurt from how aroused I was. Jacob finally circled my clit with the tip of his tongue, drawing it out of its delicate hood, and it was so good I felt like sobbing.

I *was* sobbing, I realized dazedly. I kept saying things I'd never said in my life. *Kiss me lick me fuck me. Make me come so hard my knees buckle.*

I began to move with him, and when he wouldn't give me exactly what I needed, drawing out the pleasure, I growled. He just laughed at me.

"I like making you suffer," he said as he thrust three fingers inside me. It didn't hurt this time. I was so wet I barely felt a twinge.

The combination of him sucking my clit and plunging his fingers inside me set me off like a rocket. I screamed, not caring that my neighbors could probably hear me. My knees did buckle, but Jacob was there to catch me.

"I got you," he said as I collapsed against his chest. "I got you." He kissed my temple and pushed my hair from my shoulder.

Once I caught my breath, I clambered on top of him, pulling his shirt from his pants and ripping it open. He laughed a little at my enthusiasm, but he didn't try to stop me. I kissed his chest, loving how his muscles rippled as I dragged my fingers across his skin. He cupped the back of my head as I explored him, groaning deep in his throat when I sucked hard on the side of his neck.

I'd never felt this wild before. Like I'd come out of my skin if I stopped touching this man who'd equally pissed me off and had somehow been exactly what I'd been looking for.

"Dani," said Jacob. He tugged on my hair. "Dandelion. I'm not fucking you on your floor for your first time."

I glanced at the hardwood. "It'd probably be kind of uncomfortable," I allowed.

Standing up, Jacob helped me up and took me to the bedroom. Even though it was my room, having him place me on my bed like the most precious cargo somehow rendered it completely different. My blue checkered duvet seemed brand-new to my eyes; the paintings on the wall I'd bought specially from IKEA seemed like the rarest of art.

Jacob undressed, his eyes hooded. He slipped off his shirt, letting it fall to the floor, before going to his belt. My heart pounded with anticipation. Although I'd already come once, I needed more. I needed his cock inside me. I needed *him* inside me.

When he was completely naked, I took him in: his wide shoulders, the divot at his waist, the slope of his hips; the strength in his thighs. I finally let myself take in his cock, which was a beautiful sight to behold. I let out a sigh of appreciation.

"Can I—" I nibbled on my bottom lip.

"You can do anything you want, as long as you're touching me."

When I took hold of his cock, I couldn't even wrap my fingers around him. My pussy ached. It felt so cliché, wondering if he would fit. But honestly—I wasn't sure if he would.

I had no idea what I was doing. I stroked him, rubbed him, felt him grow, to my astonishment. When I leaned down to lick the crown and tasted the bead of moisture there, I suddenly found myself flat on my back and Jacob climbing over me.

"Did I do something wrong?"

"I'm not coming in your hand." He pushed my legs apart and settled between them. "I'm coming inside this pussy, like I've dreamed of doing for so long."

He kissed me, and I could feel the head of his cock glance over my pussy. I squirmed, worry pushing through the pleasure. "Wait—wait," I gasped.

"What?"

"I just don't think—" I swallowed. "I don't think you'll fit."

I could tell Jacob was trying his hardest not to laugh. I

smacked him on the chest when his lips twitched. "I'm serious!"

"You do know how this works, don't you?"

"Don't be rude. I'm a virgin, not an idiot."

"Of course not." He sobered. "You're one of the smartest people I've ever met." He sucked on my bottom lip before nipping it. Reaching around me, he unhooked my bra and slipped it from my shoulders. "Much better." After he'd looked his fill of my breasts, he said, "Do you trust me to make sure you're ready?"

Trust—something I wasn't very good at. But in that moment, I wanted to trust him. I nodded, letting myself be taken care of by someone else for a change.

Jacob hitched my legs up, opening me up further, and his cock pressed against my entrance. I stiffened. It wasn't that it hurt; it was just strange.

"You have to relax, sweetheart."

"You wouldn't be relaxed with Godzilla trying to fuck you," I grumbled.

Jacob laughed silently, but the movement only pushed him further inside me. He groaned; I groaned.

"You're so tight. God, Dani. You're amazing. I love to feel you bare around me."

His cock pushed inside me until I felt so full, I couldn't breathe. It burned, and in a brief moment, the sharp pain made me squeak.

"I'm sorry." He kissed my forehead; he kissed my nose, then my lips. "Are you okay?"

I flexed my muscles around the intrusion of his cock, which made him grunt. He was stuffed inside me, and it was the most extraordinary feeling, having a man inside me for the first time. It was thrilling and unbearably intimate. I felt like a part of me had fused with him irrevocably.

"Yes." I arched. I needed movement, friction. Not this stillness. "Move, move, move." I dug my nails into his shoulders.

He didn't need me to say anything else. Pulling out, he slammed back into me. Our hips met, our mouths crashing together, as he pounded into my pussy and claimed not just my innocence, but my heart and soul, too.

Hooking my legs over his arms, he gave himself leverage to increase the speed of his thrusts. His cock pistoned into me with relentless speed. The pain that I'd felt had melted away, and the only thing I felt now was molten pleasure moving through my veins.

"Fuck, Dani. Fuck, fuck, fuck." Jacob was incoherent now. His usual aplomb had melted away, and it only turned me on further. I had done this to him: me, Dandelion Wright. It was almost as extraordinary as the fact that he was the one taking my virginity.

He reached down and began to rub my clit. "You need to come for me, because I can't last much longer." His voice was a growl.

It was too much: his thumb, his cock, the smell of sex and sweat, the sound of my headboard banging against the wall. I tightened around him and came again, my pussy spasming. I cried out in a hoarse voice.

Jacob slammed into me one last time before his cock twitched inside me, and he groaned my name. He filled me with his seed until I was sure I couldn't contain it all. I hadn't realized how much of a turn-on it would be to have a man lose control and come inside me like this, marking me as his.

The moment Jacob pulled out of me, leaving me bereft,

our gazes locked. His cheeks were flushed, and sweat beaded on his forehead. He was unbearably handsome yet vulnerable, too, and I realized that I'd been so very, very stupid.

Because in that moment, I knew that I was in love with him.

CHAPTER EIGHTEEN

What was the protocol when a guy slept over? Did you make him breakfast? Or would that be acting like we were in a relationship?

It was close to 6:00 AM. I needed to be at Buds and Blossoms by nine, but I was tempted to tell Judith I'd be in later. I was busy staring at the sleeping man in my bed.

I'd always thought it was creepy that sparkly vampire Edward would just sit and watch Bella sleep. Probably because he didn't ask her first, but at the moment, I understood the appeal.

In the middle of the night, I'd gotten up to pee and had been surprised to find blood smeared between my thighs. I was sore, but not enough that I would've thought I'd bled. It was so primal, the mixture of semen and blood having dried on my thighs, Jacob's come still dripping from my pussy, that I felt myself growing aroused. Maybe it'd been because I'd felt like Jacob had marked me as his own. I'd almost wanted to wake Jacob up for a second round, but I had a feeling I needed to give my body a little more time to recover.

Jacob's shoulder rose and fell with his breaths, and his hair was roughed up from sleep. Or from me running my fingers through it. I wanted to kiss his shoulder, but I didn't want him to wake up. Not quite yet.

I felt like my heart was going to burst through my chest like that creepy monster in *Alien,* except it would be a more romantic explosion. I wanted to explode all over Jacob like the lovesick idiot I was.

I'd dreamed of having sex for so long, but the real deal had been so much more than I could've expected. It had been real because in dreams, you couldn't really feel the texture of someone's skin. You couldn't taste the salt on someone's upper lip as he kissed you. You couldn't hear the way he said your name right before he came. You definitely couldn't feel the pulsing hardness of a cock almost breaking you open, and yet, somehow, putting you back together again in a strange way.

And you couldn't fall in love with a dream. Jacob had been my dream for many years; having him as my possible reality was like the difference between seeing in black and white and seeing in full color. The entire array of the rainbow was now before me, and it overwhelmed me.

Jacob stirred. I watched him come awake, turning over to look at the ceiling before he saw me. Then he smiled. And my heart flipped over in my chest.

"Good morning," he rumbled.

"Hi." I snuggled into his chest. "Did you sleep okay?"

"Like the dead." He stroked my arm. "Last night was…" He trailed off.

"Amaze-balls? Orgasmically ridiculous?"

"I was going to say 'great,' but I think those descriptions work better."

153

He kissed me. Soon, I deepened the kiss, not caring that I was sore and should probably wait for more amaze-balls sexy-times, when my stomach growled.

"Well, I guess I'm making breakfast," I said.

Kevin was waiting at his food bowl. When he saw Jacob, he didn't hiss, at least. He just swished his tail and looked disgruntled. Normally, Kevin slept with me during the night. He'd probably be pissed at me for a day or two.

I guessed that was the price you paid when you fell for a guy and he stayed over: your cat got jealous and started planning your demise.

I made us eggs and bacon, giving Kevin a few bites of bacon to appease him, the little monster. As I was scrambling the eggs, Jacob kept looking at my floral arrangement that I was going to enter into the competition.

I'd finally decided to give into my natural instinct to do something a bit avant-garde that my dad would probably hate, but the moment I'd begun putting together this design, I knew in my gut that it was right for me. An arrangement of golden-red ranunculus and large fern leaves that didn't follow a perfect curve but instead stuck out at various points.

"I've never seen anything like this," said Jacob as he moved closer to look at the arrangement. "The dying fern leaves with the brown tips..." He shook his head. "Only you would think of something like that."

I smiled, way too pleased by his compliment. "We'll see if I can win this time. I'd really love the prize money." I sighed at the thought of it.

"What would you do with it, if you won?"

"You'll probably think it's stupid," I hedged.

"I doubt that."

I began to plate our breakfasts. Where once I would never have told Jacob anything about design or running a shop, now I felt like we were partners in crime. I felt like I could trust him with this idea that my dad had never understood.

"I want to expand the store so we can teach classes and workshops," I said as I sat down at my kitchen table. "It's always been a dream of mine."

Jacob gave me an odd look. "Why would that be stupid?"

"It's not. It's just that my dad would rather keep Buds and Blossoms only about selling flowers." I shrugged, stabbing at a bite of scrambled eggs. "It's probably why he resisted having me take it over, because I would do something crazy like teach classes." I widened my eyes dramatically.

Jacob chuckled. "I think that's what parents are for. To act like change is the end of the world."

"Your parents still don't like that you're helping with Flowers, huh?"

Jacob shrugged. "They've come around to it, finally. The grumbling has cut back from once a day to once every other day."

I gave Kevin another bite of bacon under the table. "I feel like if I can win the competition, I can show my dad that I'm serious, you know? I think he believes I just want to expand on a whim, even though I've been talking about it for ages."

Jacob was chewing on a piece of bacon before saying, "I'm going to be at the convention, too. Forgot to tell you."

"Oh."

Was it silly that I felt a little hurt that he hadn't told me? I'd told him how important this competition was to me. The fact that he was going to be there seemed like a big detail to forget. Then again, we weren't *dating*. We were just…having explosive sex together.

"Do you want to share a hotel room?" I said. "I mean, to save money. Not because I'm hoping the hotel doesn't have your reservation again."

Jacob got up to take his plate to the sink. "I already have a room."

I flushed to the roots of my hair, like I'd misstepped somehow. Did he regret last night? That thought alone was enough to bring my breakfast back up.

He returned to the table with two mugs of coffee, including creamer and sugar. "I got a hotel room ages ago," he said by way of explanation, "and anyway, you'll just distract me."

I was partially mollified. "Because I'll hog the bathroom so much that you won't have time to brush your teeth, and then you'll have such bad breath that no one will buy anything from you and you'll gain a reputation as Halitosis Jacob?"

"Wouldn't happen. I'd get some of those breath strips. No one would be the wiser that I hadn't brushed my teeth."

I clucked my tongue. "My evil plans, foiled again."

Kevin came up to the table and stretched before letting out a loud meow. To my surprise, he didn't start tapping his paw against my leg for more bacon: he tapped Jacob. And kept tapping him when Jacob didn't do as he asked.

"You better give him some bacon, or he'll never leave you alone," I said, sipping my coffee. "Don't get between Kevin and his bacon." I chuckled at the pun.

Jacob gave Kevin a piece of bacon, and as the cat ate the bit of crispy meat, Jacob was able to scratch Kevin behind his ears.

They were such a funny contrast—a one-eyed, three-legged cat and this beautiful golden man—that I didn't know if I wanted to keep laughing or shed a tear. Mostly my heart felt dangerously squishy watching Jacob winning over my misanthropic cat.

"How did you end up with a cat like him?" said Jacob as Kevin went to sleep on top of his cat tree.

"I had planned to get a kitten. With four legs and two eyes, you know. But when I got to the shelter, I saw this poor cat who'd had a hard life but who still had a lot of love to give. So I ended up going home with Kevin. Even better, he was on sale because black cats are harder to adopt, let alone ones missing various body parts."

"You're amazing."

I started in surprise. "Me? No, I'm not. I'm pretty average."

"You're the least average woman I've ever met. The crazy thing is, you can't see it for yourself." Jacob kept looking at my arrangement as proof of his statement.

I was talented in that arena: I wasn't going to deny that. Having Jacob recognize that meant more to me than words could convey. Oh, my treacherous heart fell more in love with him in that second than it ever had when I'd been convinced I loved him as a kid. I'd gotten to see *him* this time, not just a fantasy mostly in my head of what it would be like to be with him.

"Thank you," I said quietly.

Finishing off my coffee, I got up and took his hand, leading him to the living room. Morning light streamed through the window decals I'd put up to give myself privacy, and it filled the room full of rainbows when the sun shone through them. I made Jacob sit on the couch, and I climbed into his lap before I kissed him.

He grunted, catching on quickly. His tongue darted into my mouth, and we kissed like that for what felt like hours. Unlike last night, when we'd been in such a hurry, this morning the kisses were slow, the touches almost lazy. Jacob stroked my breast through the tank top I'd thrown on before I'd fallen asleep. I didn't think I'd ever get used to sleeping naked.

"I like you like this," he said, sucking on my neck. His morning beard scraped against my skin.

"Sitting on your lap?"

"Yes. But in the light. Now I can really see you."

He pushed my tank top down, exposing my breasts. Pinching one nipple, he sucked the other into his mouth with the perfect amount of pressure that had me rocking into his lap. He was only wearing boxers, and his erection grew with each swivel of my hips.

I'd always thought of myself as average in terms of my looks, but I felt beautiful as Jacob stroked my back and kissed my breasts. I sucked in a breath when he blew cool air on my nipples, making them pucker.

"Are you too sore?" He palmed my pussy through my panties. "I'm not sure I can stop myself from being inside you, even if you say yes."

I moaned when he stroked through my folds. I was sore, but I didn't care. It was the kind of pain after a good, long workout: satisfying and proof that you'd done something worthwhile. Besides, Jacob's fingers were already making me so wet I could hear the sounds my pussy made when he inserted his index finger inside me.

"This perfect little pussy," he breathed against my neck, "I love how you grip my finger and my cock. Like you never want me to leave."

"I don't." I arched when he tapped my clit. "I don't want you to leave."

"If I could, I'd stay inside this pussy every hour of every day." His words washed over me like the heat from a sauna. "I wouldn't move, though. I'd just stay inside you, and when you'd beg me in that voice of yours when you're desperate and you're mad that you're so desperate——"

"I have no idea what you mean——" My voice squeaked as he rubbed my clit hard for a second before going back to gentler strokes.

"As I was saying." I could feel his smile against my throat. "I'd wait until you were clawing at me, and your pussy was pulsing around my cock, telling me that you had to come. And I'd let you—but not quickly. I'd just barely massage your clit, my cock growing inside your tight pussy every time you said my name, until you exploded around me, drenching me completely."

I was already so close. I was shaking with need. I'd never thought I would've liked dirty talk, but fuck me, I *loved* it. Even if it made me squirm and blush, I didn't care.

I reached inside Jacob's boxers and squeezed his cock, stroking him from root to tip. His jaw clenched with every pump of my hand. Even though I wanted him inside me, it was a major turn-on to have him at my mercy.

"You're a fast learner," he said. He bucked when I fondled his balls with my other hand. "*Shit.* Dani."

I kept pumping him because I wanted to see him lose it. He didn't stop me like he had last night, and I was glad. I kept stroking him, watching him pant and his muscles bunch. With a shout, he came, his seed coating my palm and dripping onto both of our legs.

I hadn't realized how *messy* sex was, but somehow what would've bothered me normally only turned me on further. It was messy and wild, and now I was so wet that my panties were soaked.

"You're still hard," I said, marveling. "I thought that wasn't a thing."

He grinned. "I'm a man of many talents."

He sounded so proud that I rolled my eyes, but soon he was stripping me of my tank top and urging me to take off the rest of my clothes. Before I maneuvered off his lap, though, he took my hand covered in his semen and used it to lube his cock, his gaze never leaving me the entire time he did so.

"Oh my God," were the only words that came to mind. "Why am I so turned on right now?"

His blue eyes were like the blue of a flame. "Take off your panties, Dani, before I tear them off."

I didn't protest. Blessedly naked, the morning light streaming in and coloring our bodies with rainbows, I sat on his lap with my legs spread wide. He took hold of his cock and pressed it against my pussy. I moaned as he sank inside me; I felt a pinch of resistance, but it disappeared just as quickly.

"Ride me." He held me by my waist to anchor me. "Fuck me, Dani."

I did. I already was. I didn't have any smooth moves, but once I started riding him, it didn't matter. I was stuffed full, until I could feel it practically in my fingertips and toes. Every time I came down, I angled my pelvis so I could get the perfect amount of pressure against my clit.

"You're so beautiful, sweetheart. Yes, just like that." Jacob palmed my ass and sucked on my breasts, which sent sensations straight to my pussy and clit.

My release slammed into me, so hard that I couldn't breathe. I shook and cried, hanging onto Jacob for dear life.

He gave me all of one second before he threw me down onto the couch and pounded into me. I could only widen my legs, taking everything he had to give me. When he came, he buried his face in my neck and filled me to the brim.

By the time we caught our breath, we both had to leave for work.

Jacob kissed me. "I'll text you," he said, caressing my cheek. He threw his suit jacket over his shoulder with a wry smile as he looked down at his outfit. "I should've brought another pair of clothes to do this walk of shame."

"But you look so sexy in a suit."

He narrowed his eyes. "Don't make me take you straight back to bed. I have work to do." He smacked my ass, kissed me one last time, and then left me feeling dazed, ecstatic, and beautifully exhausted.

CHAPTER NINETEEN

It was hard to concentrate when your brain was reminding you that you'd had sex last night. And that you'd had sex this morning. And that it would very much like you to have more sex.

Sex sex sex sex sex sex SEXXXXXXX went my brain that Saturday morning. It was pretty much an endless stream of porno, except it was featuring me and Jacob.

When my first customer came in, she wanted to buy some peonies. Except my brain heard *penis*, and then my brain thought, *I LOVE PENISES!* And for a moment my body got very excited, too. Until my customer looked at me strangely, as if she knew my mind was a nonstop loop of Pornhub, and I realized that I hadn't said a word to her.

Like I said: way harder to concentrate than I would've expected.

During a lull, I checked my phone and saw that Anna had texted me a bunch of times last night, but my phone had been on silent so I hadn't heard them.

7:05 PM: Want to get drinks tonight?

7:30 PM: Where are you? You better not be dead.

8:16 PM: WHY ARE YOU IGNORING ME. Fine, be a bitch-face.

8:41 PM: I'm assuming your phone is broken otherwise I'm kicking your ass tomorrow.

10:14 PM: I really hope you aren't dead, though.

"So you are alive," said Anna on the first ring. "Or you're Dani's kidnapper and are demanding a hefty ransom."

"How could a kidnapper use my phone when it's locked?" I countered.

"Easy. Use your fingerprint to unlock it. If you were tied up, you wouldn't have a choice."

I didn't really want to ask why Anna knew so much about this subject. "Well, I'm not dead." I took a deep breath. "Actually, Jacob came over last night."

"Is that code for, 'he came over to talk about growing potatoes' or something boring? Or are you telling me something else?"

"No potatoes were involved." I lowered my voice, even though no one was here to listen. "We slept together."

I held the phone away from my ear right before Anna screeched like a banshee.

"You little slut! You had sex and didn't text me right after?"

I didn't even need to put my phone on speaker to hear her. "I'm not going to text you at two in the morning to give you the nitty-gritty details."

"Give me the details now. And I mean *everything*."

Despite Anna's demands otherwise, I didn't give her every

single detail, although I did give in and tell her how much Jacob was packing (re: a lot). She screeched again when I told her that tidbit and I was pretty sure my eardrums were bleeding from it.

"Wait, hold up," she said, "why was he wearing a suit? Did he have some fancy flower meeting to go to?"

"Oh, I forgot that part. He came here as my prom date, to make up for the fact that he stood me up."

Anna was silent for so long that I thought the call had dropped.

"Dandelion Nicole Wright, are you seriously telling me that Jacob West got dressed up in a tuxedo, brought you a bouquet and a corsage, and danced with you to Taylor Swift last night?"

"Yeah. Is that a bad thing?"

"Bad? Woman, he's in love with you."

I laughed when she said the words, but soon I had to sit down because my knees had turned watery. I was the one in love with Jacob; that love had always been unrequited. *Always.*

"He's not in love with me," I protested weakly.

"No guy does something like that if he doesn't have feelings for you. Come on, Dani. You're a smart girl, and you know I don't bullshit."

"He didn't say anything about it."

"Well, to be fair, neither have you." I could see Anna rolling her eyes. "You're both idiots. Honestly."

The door chime rang, signaling a customer. After I told Anna goodbye, I forced my attention away from our conversation, but it was nearly impossible.

Jacob, in love with me? It was such an extraordinary idea that the remote thought that it could be true overwhelmed me.

I'd gotten so used to the idea that he'd never want me. But he did want me, didn't he? At least physically. And he seemed to care about my well-being.

Love, though? That seemed like a stretch to me, yet I couldn't stop the excitement bubbling up inside me.

Maybe Anna was right. Maybe he was falling in love with me.

I was so preoccupied that I didn't hear my next customer come in while I was trimming fresh-cut tulips in the back.

"Dani? You here?" It was Mari, thank God.

"Back here!"

I wanted to ask Mari's advice. She knew how men worked. If she thought along the same lines as Anna, then there was a good chance Jacob did love me. I let out a little squeal and ended up cutting one of the tulip stems way too short.

"I'm glad you're here—" I was saying, only to stop when I saw my sister's face. "What is it?"

I'd never seen Mari like this: without makeup, her hair in a messy ponytail, her eyes bloodshot and her face red. She was even wearing torn-up sweats and an old t-shirt that had paint splatters on it. I didn't even know my sister owned sweats.

Her bottom lip quivered. Then to my utter amazement, she burst into noisy sobs.

I acted quickly: after putting up the CLOSED sign and locking the front door, I returned to the back and had Mari sit down. We didn't have tissues back here, but we at least had a roll of paper towels.

"Tell me what happened," I said. "It isn't Mom or Dad, is it?"

Mari ripped off a paper towel and blew her nose into it so loudly that I would've laughed if she weren't so miserable.

"No, no. They're fine." She took another towel and wiped her eyes, but the tears kept coming. "It's David."

"Is he okay? Did something happen?"

Mari started crying so hard that she couldn't speak. Worry assailed me. Had David wrecked his brand-new Prius and was now clinging to life? But, no, Mari wouldn't be here if he were in the hospital. She would've called me.

After a few more hiccups and sobs, Mari said in gasps, "David. Cheated. On. Me."

I was almost sure I'd misunderstood her. *David* had cheated on her? Boring, stick-in-the-mud, IRAs-are-so-exciting David? I couldn't believe it because what woman would throw herself at a guy like him? Nobody was that desperate.

Then again, Mari loved him. Or had loved him, based on the anger suffusing her face right now. He must've had some qualities that had attracted her to him.

"Are you sure he's cheating on you?" I said. "Have you talked to him? Maybe it's a misunderstanding."

"I saw him fucking another woman," spat Mari. "I think that's more than enough proof." She wiped at her eyes, rage flashing across her face. "We bought those stupid buttons, you know? Because he didn't like it when I didn't want to have sex. But lately, he hadn't been pressing his at all. I knew something was up. I thought maybe he was bored, so I got new lingerie and went over to his apartment."

Mari swallowed hard. "I heard a noise from his bedroom, but it never occurred to me he'd be cheating on me. I thought he was moving furniture around." She barked out a laugh. "I came inside his room, and some woman was on her knees on his bed as he fucked her from behind. And he'd always told me he didn't like doggy style."

It was such an unsettling image that I had to sit down. "Then what happened?"

"Basically lots of shouting, the woman demanding to know who I was. Apparently, David had neglected to tell her he was engaged. He ran after me, begging me to forgive him." She held up her left hand. "I threw his ring in his face and told him to go fuck himself."

The anger diffused, replaced with grief. The tears started up again. "What did I do wrong?" she whispered. "I thought we were going to be so happy. We'd just talked about whether or not we wanted a vegan option at our wedding."

I wrapped my arms around my sister as she started crying again. This time, her sobs were whimpers, and it broke my heart. I might not have liked David, but I'd wanted to for Mari's sake. Now I just wanted to find him and run him over with my car very slowly.

Mari finally pulled away and wiped at her face with one of the many paper towels she'd torn off the roll. "What am I going to do? We already sent out the wedding invitations. The venue is booked, my dress is ordered." She paled. "We're going to have to tell two hundred people that the wedding is off."

"Don't think about that right now. Besides, maybe you and David will make up," I said, even though I wasn't at all convinced he could make it up to my sister.

Mari scowled. "There's nothing he could say that would make me forgive him. He keeps calling me and leaving me voicemails, saying how sorry he is."

She showed me her phone, which had so many message

notifications that you had to scroll for a while to see them all. "At least he feels bad?" I said.

"He's not going to get a cookie for feeling guilty that he got caught." Mari wrapped her arms around her middle, tears leaking from her eyes, but she brushed them away. "Tell me something good. I don't want to keep thinking about this. My head hurts from crying so much."

I'd wanted to tell her about me and Jacob, but that seemed rather cruel, given the circumstances. How could I tell her about how happy I was with Jacob when her fiancé had betrayed her like this? It would just be rubbing it in her face.

"I finished my design for the competition," I supplied.

"That's great. Tell me about it."

I did, in way too much detail, but I knew that Mari just needed me to talk. I told her about how I'd gone back and forth on what I wanted to do, how I'd decided to do something that wasn't the standard kind of arrangement that you'd see in a competition like this. She asked questions, but I could tell she was far away.

I realized this was the first time in recent memory that Mari had ever come to me with a problem. She'd always seemed like she had her life together, even when we'd been kids. She was beautiful, talented, successful. She had who we thought was a great fiancé. She was going to get married and live in a nice house with her nice husband and have nice children while she worked at her nice job.

But I knew now that that niceness had been a facade. I had a hard time imagining that this had been the first indication that there was trouble brewing in her relationship with David. I'd been too self-centered to pry deeper, though. I'd assumed everything was perfect with her because I felt so imperfect in comparison.

"Did you show Jacob your design?" said Mari.

I had returned to trimming tulips, and I almost cut another one in half at her remark. "What?"

"Oh, come on. There aren't any secrets in this neighborhood. Edith saw Jacob coming out of your apartment this morning." Mari smiled wryly. "I'm going to assume he wasn't over there playing Yahtzee with you."

"Close. Monopoly."

Mari threw a tulip at my head. "Were you seriously not going to tell me about you two?" Hurt sounded in her voice. "Or did you just not want to tell me?"

I stared at her in surprise. "Of course I wanted to tell you, but I wasn't going to rub it in your face, either, after what you just told me. That seems kind of heartless."

"I'd rather hear good news than wallow in my bad news."

I was still wary of saying too much that would make Mari feel badly, but I told her everything I felt comfortable sharing.

"Anna thinks he's in love with me," I ended. "I told her that she's crazy."

Mari had propped her chin on her hand. "He might be, though. Men don't do things like that for women they just consider friends with benefits."

My heart started pounding hard. "What should I do?"

"Ask him. Be honest." She smiled, although I could see sadness around the edges. "Tell him how you feel, even if it rocks the boat. It feels like the hardest thing ever, but not saying anything will only make things worse in the long run."

We both jumped when someone knocked on the front door. Had an hour really passed already?

After telling Mari goodbye and hugging her, I ended up being busy with customers the rest of the afternoon. But even as I gave suggestions for arrangement styles and types of bouquets and corsages, I couldn't help but wonder if this David thing had been a sign from the universe.

Did I risk everything and tell Jacob that I loved him? Or did I keep it to myself, because even seemingly solid relationships like Mari and David's could come crashing down at any time, let alone whatever it was Jacob and I were doing?

All I knew right then was that, no matter which choice I made, there was a good chance heartbreak would be the result.

CHAPTER TWENTY

The next few days were a whirlwind of preparation, not just for the competition, but with creating bouquets for a wedding for that Sunday. Judith had worked with me on tons of weddings, but she'd never gone to one on her own. I wanted to make sure everything went as smoothly as possible while I was gone.

"It'll be fine," said Judith for the thousandth time. "You aren't going to the moon. I can call you if I need to."

"I know. I trust you and Will." I forced a smile onto my face. "I'm just nervous. Sorry if I'm taking it out on you."

Judith told me that I could buy her a drink when I got back, to which I agreed readily. I'd probably need a drink or five once this competition was over. Not only did I need to make sure Buds and Blossoms was running during my absence, but my dad had come by that morning to see my arrangement. He'd been decidedly unenthusiastic with my design.

"Honey, you're so talented, but I thought you wanted to win," he'd said. He'd sounded genuinely flummoxed. "This isn't a winning design." He'd then begun to give me suggestions how to fix it, as if I hadn't realized my design was actually a hot-mess.

I'd gritted my teeth, told my dad it was too late to change it, and had stewed in my frustration and hurt for the rest of the day. It had only been Jacob's texts, reminding me that we were going to be in Los Angeles together within two days, that had gotten me through the weekend.

On Monday, Jacob and I were eating dinner together at an Italian restaurant off Melrose. It was still warm outside, even though the sun had started to set. I'd been to Los Angeles many times, but I always forgot how clear the blue skies were here in Southern California. Pacific Northwest living tended to make you think everywhere else was cloudy all the time.

While we waited for our food, Jacob was oddly quiet, and I kept having to repeat my questions.

"Is something the matter?" I finally said after we'd gotten our meals. I'd given in and ordered fettuccine alfredo because I'd barely eaten all day.

"No." He smiled, but it didn't reach his eyes. "Are you ready for tomorrow?"

"I think so. My arrangement got here fine, and I got to check it over. I'm always afraid the courier will drop it or drive over potholes on purpose."

"They would be a terrible courier if they did."

"I've had couriers who I'm pretty sure did just that." I winced at the memory. "I remember once when I was in high school, I got to this competition in Atlanta and half my arrangement had fallen off. I don't know how I managed to fix it in time. I was basically a sobbing mess at the end."

"Did you win?"

I smiled wryly. "No. Second place."

"Do you think you would have otherwise?"

I shrugged. "Maybe, but the girl who did win was better than me, honestly. Getting second place that time was pretty much a miracle."

Jacob drank his wine, watching me the entire time. I mirrored him and raised an eyebrow for good measure. He could be as mysterious as he wanted, but I was pretty sure I could see through him. I wasn't going to take the facade as truth anymore. I'd done that with Mari; I wasn't going to do the same with Jacob.

"How's your dad?" I said. I twirled a bite of pasta around my fork, and then couldn't help but moan at the taste. "Geez, that's good. Don't watch me eat because I'm going to inhale this."

"He's not doing great, honestly."

I stared at him in surprise. "What? Why didn't you tell me?"

"Because I didn't want to burden you with that information."

"Well, that's a stupid reason. Is this recent? I thought he was recovering?"

Jacob sighed, pushing his fingers through his hair. "He is. Was. But he was getting really frustrated at not being able to move around like he used to. He used to run marathons, go to the gym every day. Now he can only hobble around with a cane."

"I'm sorry. That has to be hard to watch."

Jacob kept talking, like he hadn't heard me. "He's not only lost his mobility, but we're coming to realize that he's lost a lot of things. Vocabulary, for one. He also tends to keep telling the same handful of stories over and over." Jacob's expression was pained. "He'd always been the strongest person I knew. After he had his stroke, my mom kept telling me I didn't need to come home, that he was fine. If I'd known…"

Guilt assailed me, because I'd been so obsessed over this competition, over my feelings for Jacob, over *myself*, that I hadn't considered that Jacob could be hurting like this. I wished he would've told me, but like Mari, had I tried to get him to tell me? Or had he felt like he couldn't tell me?

"You can't blame yourself," I said, taking his hand and squeezing it. "Your parents probably wanted to protect you. They're weird like that."

"But I'm not a kid. They just didn't want to admit the truth."

"I get that. Sometimes it's hardest to admit the truth to yourself, let alone to people you love."

At the mention of love, I colored, glad that it was dark enough now that Jacob couldn't see me blushing. Did he know how I felt about him? I almost hoped that he did while I hoped like hell that he didn't.

Jacob clenched his jaw, and something made his eyes stormy. I wondered if there was more that he wasn't telling me.

"I hope you know you can talk to me about whatever," I said.

In a flash, he looked stricken, but it disappeared quickly. That aplomb he was so good at smoothed across his handsome features. "I want to take you back to the hotel and see if you're wearing any panties under your dress," he said in a low voice that turned my insides to liquid.

"Then you're just going to have to wait." I made a note to

take off my panties in the restaurant bathroom to surprise him before we got back to the hotel.

JACOB HAD JUST SHUT the door of his hotel room behind him when he practically pounced on me, kissing me with a wildness that stunned me. His hands were seemingly everywhere at once—my breasts, my ass, my arms, my mound—that I couldn't keep up with his movements. He pinned me against the wall and wouldn't let me move, not that I wanted to.

I ran my fingers through his hair. I tasted wine on his tongue, and his cock was an iron bar against my belly. When he pushed the skirt of my dress up and discovered I wasn't wearing any panties, his eyes widened slightly.

"You naughty girl," he whispered, parting my pussy lips to find me already dripping. "Were you soaking wet while we sat and ate dinner, your pussy bare under your dress?"

I whimpered as he petted me. "Jacob—"

"I know what you need. Hold your dress up."

He went to his knees and roughly widened my legs before he began to suckle my clit, his tongue licking inside my sheath. My head knocked against the wall, fire rushing through my veins. I took hold of his hair and tried to guide him where I wanted, but he just laughed darkly and did what he wanted.

"I could eat this pussy every hour of every day," he whispered heatedly. "I love how you drip into my mouth when you're close."

I could never draw enough oxygen into my lungs when Jacob played with my body like this. He listened to every sigh, every moan, watched me arch and buck, and he seemed to read my mind with every stroke of his tongue.

I fucked his mouth as best as I could when I was holding my dress up with one hand and Jacob held me against the wall. He lifted my right leg onto his shoulder, opening me further. Rubbing my clit at the same time he tongue-fucked my sheath, I came within a millisecond. I bit down on my lip until it bled to keep from screaming.

"There you go. You taste so good. Your pussy is my favorite."

I giggled, boneless, as he helped me strip out of my dress and bra. By then, I was able to undo his belt and take hold of his cock, which was already weeping at the tip.

"I like your cock, too," I said. "It's my favorite."

"It'd better be."

I licked the tip, loving the salty taste of him. I went down on my knees and took as much of him into my mouth as I could manage.

"Fuck, Dani." Jacob stroked my hair. "Seeing you on your knees with my cock in your pretty mouth…"

He was too big for me to take him completely, and I was too much of a novice to know how to deep throat. But Jacob didn't push me—he never did. He let me explore and figure things out on my own, sometimes giving some instruction when I was at a loss, other times simply encouraging me. I couldn't have asked for a better instructor in the art of sex. My only regret was that we'd wasted so much time *not* doing this, disregarding the fact that we'd been on opposite sides of the country for the last nine years.

I felt him grow larger, and when he bumped the back of

my throat, I pulled free with a gasp. I coughed a little and my eyes watered.

"You okay?" He lifted my chin, wiping the saliva off of my lip.

"Yeah, that's never going to fit all the way."

He grinned. "Never say never. You'll get there."

I shivered from the promise in his eyes. Soon his grin faded, and before I knew it, he was naked, we were on the bed together, and he was thrusting inside my pussy. I was still sensitive from my orgasm, and I gasped when he filled me to the hilt.

He stopped, but I arched my hips. "Why did you stop?"

"You sounded like I hurt you."

"No, no, it doesn't hurt, it hasn't hurt in a while, if you don't start moving I'm going to *murder* you—"

He chuckled, pulled out, and slammed back into me. I groaned. He fucked me with relentless speed, the headboard banging against the wall. I had the stray thought that the hotel would be pretty pissed if their ugly paintings fell off the wall because we were having such intense sex.

I started laughing, which made Jacob stop. "What's so funny?" He looked on the verge of being offended.

I touched his jaw, smiling. "Nothing. I mean, it's not you. It's me. I'm dumb. Oh, why did you stop?" I pushed at his chest, clawing at him like a kitten. "I was close to coming again." I sounded like a whiny child and I didn't even care.

In a move that left me breathless, he turned me over onto my stomach and pinned me to the bed. He slid his cock inside me—slowly, because in this position, I was tighter than ever.

"What makes you think you have any control?" he growled. He held still, my pussy fluttering around his cock.

"Because you keep telling me what to do, and it's not going to work, sweetheart."

"Because you keep stopping!" I wanted to claw his face off, the jerk-face.

"How about you behave for once?"

I scowled into the comforter, considering telling him to eat a dick. Until he began to thrust again. Apparently, I would do anything for an orgasm, especially when it was Jacob giving me one.

With me pinned by his body, his legs keeping mine wide open, he was the one in complete control. And I *loved* it. He plunged into me in a steady rhythm, ignoring me begging him to go faster. He just laughed at me again because he was the fucking worst and the most amazing at the same time.

My release was just out of reach. I tightened around him, and as he kept filling me, it was so good it almost hurt. I buried my face in the sheets and started screaming as my orgasm ripped through me.

"Fuck!" Jacob roared and came at the same time as me. He gushed inside me in seemingly endless spurts. When he finally pulled out of me, I could feel his come dripping onto my thighs and the comforter.

I couldn't move. I could only stare into Jacob's flushed face, watching the rise and fall of his chest as I tried to catch my breath.

To my surprise, tears sprang to my eyes. How did I describe this intensity building inside me? I felt like I'd been turned inside out. Jacob stroked my spine as I closed my eyes and tried to calm my pounding heart.

Maybe it was the afterglow, or the fact that I couldn't hold the words back anymore. Maybe I'd gone temporarily insane.

But the words, "I love you," flew from my lips to rest between us like a curious bird.

Jacob didn't say anything. His forehead creased, then he got up and went to the bathroom. I stared at his naked back, the ripple of his ass as he walked.

He returned with a wet washcloth and cleaned us both. I blushed, and I blushed because he hadn't said anything to my declaration. *God, I was an idiot.*

I found my bra in the corner, and I put it on so hastily that I missed a hook. Throwing my dress over my head, I was about to grab my purse when Jacob said, "Where are you going?"

I couldn't look at him. If I did, I'd start sobbing. "It's late," I managed in a voice that was somehow still steady. "I should go to my room. We have to be up early."

It wasn't really late—only 10:00 PM. We didn't really have to get up that early, either. But Jacob didn't try to poke holes in my lie, and strangely, that hurt most of all.

He just said, "Okay. See you tomorrow."

And I left, feeling like my heart had been shredded.

CHAPTER TWENTY-ONE

I woke up the next morning with a giant headache like I was hung over. I'd barely slept, and I'd stopped myself from going back to Jacob's room, banging on the door, and demanding to know what the hell his problem was.

Except that meant having to hear the words I didn't want to hear: I don't love you. *Sorry, Dani. This has just been a fling. You knew that, right?*

I forced my mind away from Jacob and his bullshit. Today was the competition. The judges would choose the winners midmorning. I was so close to that prize money and contract that I could smell it. I was immensely proud of my arrangement, despite my dad not being a fan of it. Even if the judges didn't like it, at least I was proud of myself and my hard work.

I left the hotel and walked to the convention center that was a block away. Since it was still early in the morning, it wasn't packed, but it would be pretty soon. I grabbed coffee and began to wander through the gardens that had been created inside the convention center itself.

Each garden was themed: a Mediterranean garden with a

portico and an orange tree; a garden from Switzerland that looked like it had been transplanted from the Alps; and a garden that was only orchids. The orchids made me wish my dad were here. Listening to him telling me about how he would've done my arrangement differently would be preferable to this melancholy over Jacob.

I didn't want to consider that the reason he hadn't said anything was because he didn't love me. I pushed that thought away, put it in a safe, locked it, and then buried it six feet under. Metaphorically speaking. Except thoughts like that have a way of becoming zombies and rising from the dead. It kept poking at me throughout the morning like a total sadist.

Later, I was considering buying a pillow shaped like a cactus when Jacob found me. I didn't know how he always managed to find me. I would've accused him putting a tracking device on my phone, except guys who looked horrified when you told them you loved them weren't particularly inclined to stalking, or so I assumed.

Jacob had bags under his eyes; I wondered if he'd slept as little as me. Good. I hoped that his coffee would always be burnt and watery, that his food would taste like buttholes, and that he always forgot to pack underwear.

"Are you going to buy that?" he said, pointing to the pillow I was holding.

I had been going to buy it, but I didn't want to prove that he'd been right about me. "No."

I walked away, but to my immense annoyance, Jacob followed me. He wrapped his hand around my elbow to get me to stop.

"Dani, we need to talk—"

"This is a change. You didn't seem all that interested in talking last night." I pulled my arm free and kept walking.

I heard Jacob swear, and I knew I was being maybe a little bit unfair. He didn't *owe* me the words "I love you." And it wasn't even that I wanted him to say them now: it was more that he hadn't said anything at all. Couldn't he have at least pulled a Han Solo and said, *I know?* That would've been preferable to what had amounted to no response.

"Wait, Dani. Come on."

I had reached the end of the row of booths, and I had to either turn around and face Jacob or stare at the wall until we both died. I decided on the latter choice. I refused to look at him.

"There are things you don't understand," said Jacob, "things that make this all really complicated."

"That is the vaguest explanation ever." I crossed my arms, hugging myself. "And tells me absolutely nothing."

"I know, I just…"

I could hear the frustration in his voice, and it took everything in me not to turn to him and say, *It's okay. Don't worry about it.* Because then we could go on doing what we'd been doing, and I could ignore that this relationship meant more to me than it did to him.

"Look, you don't have to explain. You don't love me. That's fine." I couldn't stop the tremor from entering my voice. "I shouldn't have thrown that at you. Just forget about it."

Like Lot's wife, I stupidly turned back to look at Jacob, and I saw hurt flash across his face. Hurt, frustration, confusion, the same emotions broiling inside me. We were mirrors of each other, and apparently incapable of explaining what we both felt.

"Ladies and gentlemen," a voice over the intercom boomed, "the floral design winners have been chosen! You can see the winning arrangements and all the entries in the atrium. Congratulations to the winners!"

"I have to go," I said, pushing past Jacob.

I heard him say something that sounded like *wait*, but I darted into the crowd before he could catch me. I practically elbowed some woman out of the way when she stopped right in front of me, I was so edgy with anticipation.

I could see that blue ribbon next to my arrangement in my mind. I could see people viewing my design and when I told them I had created it, everyone would tell me congratulations, complimenting me on how different and brilliant my design was. That first prize was mine—mine, mine, mine—

They say when you almost die, your life flashes before your eyes. I didn't almost die when I entered that atrium, but my brain flashed through a hodgepodge of memories before I could put words to what I was seeing.

I saw myself a kindergartener, pulling up dandelions. I saw Kate as a little kid pulling apart daisies I'd put in my window. I saw Jacob driving off with Tiffany that fateful night nine years ago. I saw Jacob as an adult before he kissed me for that first time.

Then my brain adjusted and I saw what was right in front of me.

My arrangement, then next to it, a red ribbon.

Second place. A red ribbon meant second.

A red ribbon meant…I'd lost.

I'd lost. *I'd motherfucking lost.*

It was easy to see who'd won, because everyone was congregated around that arrangement. I hadn't stopped to look at the entries earlier because I'd wanted to wait until they'd announced the winners. Now I almost wished I had looked at them, because then my curiosity wouldn't need to be assuaged.

My first thought when I saw the winning arrangement was that it was absolutely beautiful. It was delicate, deceptively simple, yet looking at it, I saw echoes—as much as you can *see* echoes.

I took in the buckeye flowers—not purple this time, but pink—and the vine of dates instead of porcelain like the arrangement I'd been working on that first time Jacob had come into Buds and Blossoms. And to top it off: Black Wizard dahlias. Everything came together with a neat little click in my brain when I saw who'd designed the arrangement.

Jacob and Kenneth West of Flowers, Seattle, WA

"Fuck," said Jacob over my shoulder.

I didn't need to look at his face now, but I did, because I was a masochist. Despite the anger—at me? Himself?—in his expression, he still managed to look absurdly handsome. I imagined clawing his eyeballs out and felt a little better.

I pushed past him. He tried to catch my arm, but I whirled on him and hissed, "Touch me again and I'll scream."

Jacob put up his hands, but he still followed me. He kept trying to get me to stop, to let him explain. When I got to my hotel room, my hands were shaking so hard that I dropped my key card on the ground. Jacob picked it up before I could and slid it into the lock, which meant that I could either leave the hotel or let him inside my room.

I let him inside because I wanted to hear him try to talk

himself out of this.

We faced each other. I felt surprisingly calm, but I knew it was false. My knees were watery, and I was close to throwing up.

"Why?" was the only word I could manage to croak. I held onto the back of a chair. "Why?"

Jacob's fists were clenched, his jaw tight. He looked ten years older in that moment. "I told them to take my name off the arrangement, Dani. I didn't want you to know—"

"You think I wouldn't have noticed that you ripped off *my* design? How stupid do you think I am?"

"I didn't have a choice. I swear to God, I didn't." He came closer to me, until I could see the stubble on his cheeks.

"What, did the mafia put a gun to your head and tell you to rip me off? Come on, Jacob. We're talking about flowers, not cocaine." I wanted to laugh, because it was absurd. We were talking about flowers, for Christ's sake. The most benign thing on this earth besides puppies and rainbows.

"No, there weren't any guns. And the mafia doesn't really care about bouquets, even though they probably would need them all the time, considering how often people get killed around them."

I wasn't in the mood for jokes. "Just tell me this: was sleeping with me required, or was that just a bonus?"

Jacob flinched. "It wasn't like that. I swear."

"Well, then, explain it to me. Maybe use simple words, though. Apparently, I'm not getting anything today."

Pushing his fingers through his hair, he said, "I came into your store that first time because I wanted to see how you guys were running it. Because it's doing well, whereas Flowers hasn't been doing great. My dad, though, he wanted to enter the competition. He used to do it all the time, but since his stroke, he couldn't put together arrangements like he used to. Not just design them, but physically put them together."

Jacob began to pace, looking rather like an agitated, golden lion. "Then I saw your arrangement, and when I told my dad about it, he was impressed. He began to use it as inspiration. He was sure we could win."

"And he was right. You did win." In a fit of rage, I picked up the phone book and threw it at Jacob's head. He ducked just in the nick of time. "You won, and I can't call it cheating because you didn't copy me exactly," I said, throwing a pad of Post-its at him this time. "How clever of you! Except I guess taking *inspiration* from me wasn't enough. How many other bits of information did you steal from us, Jacob?"

At this point, I was right in front of him, and I grabbed fistfuls of his shirt. He didn't try to stop me. He just stood straight and tall, and I wanted to punch through his emotional armor. I wanted him on his knees, begging me for forgiveness.

"I'm curious, though," I said, "what was the point of fucking me? Wait!" My eyes widened mock-dramatically. "You were trying to get close to me to learn all my secrets. You thought, if I finger-bang her, she'll tell me everything. It's a foolproof plan! Who knew running flower shops could be so cutthroat?"

"That's where you're wrong."

"You're not doing a great job of convincing me."

Apparently he'd had enough of me throwing things at him and wrinkling his shirt. He grabbed my hands and pushed them behind my back. "I never expected any of this to happen, okay? I went to your store that first day for one reason and I ended up going back for another. For *you*, Dani."

His grip was tight, almost hurting me, but I was glad of it. It kept my anger hot enough that I wouldn't start crying.

"After that night in Vancouver, I told my dad I wasn't going to help him anymore. It was wrong, but it didn't matter. It was too late," he said.

"How sad for you."

Jacob backed me up until I ran into the bed, and somehow, he was on top of me, pinning me down. I tried to kick him, but he was way bigger and stronger than me.

I spat, "You could've tried being honest with me. Did you ever think about that? If you had come clean weeks ago, I might have forgiven you!"

"You're a liar." Red slashed his cheeks. "You remember that conversation we had? About how you don't trust people? It would've given you the perfect reason to call this whole thing off. You would've felt justified, because I would've been just another person who'd disappointed you. But I wasn't going to let you run from me."

I arched my back, my neck, trying to put even an inch of space between us. "Fuck you, Jacob. Don't put this on me! You're the one who lied!"

"I did. I motherfucking lied because I couldn't let you go. Is that what you wanted to hear?"

Tears sprang to my eyes. I closed them, the hot tears trickling to my temples. "Why?" I gasped.

"Because I fell in love with you. Christ, Dani, *I love you*."

It was strange, hearing those words, because I'd dreamed of hearing them for years and years. Yet now, they were completely hollow. My heart didn't explode with happiness. My heart only hardened.

"Get off of me," I hissed. I dug my nails into his back. "Get. Off. Of. Me."

It took him a long moment, but he finally let me go. I scrambled away from him.

I gasped out, "You lied to me. You stole from me. You used me." I listed his sins, enjoying the way he winced when I said each one. "And now you want me to forget about all of that because you love me? Your arrogance is astonishing."

"You lied, too."

I stared up at him in shock.

"You tell everyone you're all about honesty, but you can't even be honest with yourself. You push people away instead of letting them be human. You put me on this pedestal when we were kids. I'm not fucking perfect." His voice rose with each word. "I knew then I couldn't be your knight in shining armor because I knew I'd fail you. Because everyone is going to fail you, eventually, because nobody can live up to your insane expectations."

I sat on the bed, stunned. I wanted to tell him he was wrong; I wanted to deny every word, but I couldn't, because it would be a lie.

"You don't get to absolve yourself and turn this on me. That's unfair. I don't expect anyone to be perfect. I just want them to tell me the fucking truth!" I let out a sob. "Just go. Leave me alone."

"Sweetheart—"

"You don't get to call me that!" I almost screamed. "Get out. Get out!"

He sighed. With one last look over his shoulder, he said, "I'm sorry."

And then he was gone.

CHAPTER TWENTY-TWO

After I got home from Los Angeles, I avoided going to my parents' house for dinner for two weeks in a row. The first week, I said I was too tired and wanted to stay home. The second week, I lied and said I had too much work to do. By the third, my mom pretty much came to my apartment and dragged me to dinner.

"You can't sit in your apartment and wallow forever," she said. "You got second place, sweetheart. That's nothing to sneeze at."

I hadn't felt all that inclined to tell her I wasn't wallowing because of my loss. That was a very tiny part of this shit situation I'd found myself in. Losing fair and square would be one thing: I'd lost before, and although it sucked, it was the nature of the game.

Losing because the guy who I'd fallen in love with had won by being a sneaky cheating asshole?

That was something else entirely.

I hadn't told anyone what had happened down in LA, not

even Anna. I preferred to believe it had never happened. If I brushed it under the rug, then it didn't exist.

But it kept coming out from under the rug and squeezing my heart until I felt like I couldn't breathe. I dreamed about Jacob—good dreams, bad dreams. Weird dreams where he transformed into a beaver and tried to destroy my house by chewing it to pieces.

I was, in a word, a wreck. But nobody seemed to notice. Like I'd done with Mari, they assumed what they saw on the surface was the truth, and they didn't feel like delving below that layer.

"Dani, pass the rolls," said my dad at dinner. I was picking at my cauliflower and farro salad; I'd probably lost five pounds in the last two weeks simply from not eating very much.

"Dani, did you hear me?" my dad said again.

My entire family stared at me: Kate with suspicion; Mari with a kind of absent interest; my mom with real concern; my dad with confusion. I watched the emotions play across their faces like a movie. I would've laughed, but nothing seemed all that funny lately. Not even dreams about Jacob as a beaver had provided more than a halfhearted chuckle when I'd woken up.

I passed the rolls, as requested. I mumbled something in reply.

"Do you know who I ran into today?" said my mom. "Heidi West. She wanted to tell you congratulations, Dani, on your getting second place." My mom wrinkled her nose. "Then she proceeded to tell me how proud she was of her son and husband for winning first place, like she wanted to lord it over me."

"Still can't believe they, of all people, won." My dad shook his head, pointing his fork at me. "I'm sorry to say, Dani, but you should've listened to me. There was no reason why you couldn't have gotten first place if you'd done something that wasn't so out there."

I gritted my teeth so hard I was pretty sure they would turn to dust in a few seconds. Mari squeezed my hand under the table, and it was only her silent sympathy that kept me from storming out of the house.

"That's not to say your design wasn't beautiful," my mom said. "You always come up with such interesting ideas. That has to count for something."

"She did get second place," supplied Kate. "So it must not have sucked that bad."

"Of course it didn't suck. Dani's designs never suck." My dad waved a hand. "But sometimes you have to fit inside the box to win the box."

"Who would want to win a box?" This from Kate.

"It's a metaphor," said Mari.

"No, it's not. At least, it's not a very good one," said Kate.

My family began to debate the merits of my design, whether anyone would want to win a box, if my dad was right, if the judges had been bribed (the Wests weren't any of our favorites, but that seemed like a stretch even to me), if it had been because Mercury had been in retrograde, as my mom believed. "It would've been better if they'd scheduled it a week later when the moon entered Aries," she said with a shake of her head.

"I can't help but wonder what they're going to do with that prize money. They could try to buy us out, you know," said my dad. "Put us out of business altogether. They've been wanting to do that since they first opened."

Anger burst inside me. I threw my fork down onto my plate, the clattering sound drawing my family's immediate attention. I stood up from my chair and gripped the edge of the table.

"Please. Stop. Talking," I eked out.

"Honey, what's wrong?" said my mom.

Tears threatened. My bottom lip wobbled. I felt so stupid, getting upset like this, that I only managed to say, "Cauliflower is the fucking worst," before I burst into tears and ran from the room.

My dad was the one who came after me. He didn't say anything, but instead ushered me to his office and shut the door to give us privacy. Pushing a box of tissues in front of me, he waited for my tears to abate, much like he used to do when I was a kid and had gotten upset that Mari had made fun of my hair or Kate had messed with my dolls.

Except my dad couldn't ground Jacob or make him buy me new dolls with his allowance. I wished I could go back to those days, when my parents could fix things for me with such ease. But I was an adult now; I couldn't climb into my dad's lap and tell him my troubles as he assured me that things would get better.

"I have a feeling this isn't about you getting second place," he said after I'd blown my nose a half-dozen times. "You never get this upset about not getting first place. I think the one time you did cry, it was because a judge dared to suggest that your arrangement wasn't symmetrical." He chuckled at the memory.

I smiled, despite my mood. "I was mad about that comment for weeks."

"You were." My dad's brow clouded with concern. "Do

you want to talk about it? I'd tell you that you don't have to say anything, but the rest of the family is going to demand to know what's going on if I don't find out."

"You guys are all a bunch of damn snoops."

"Only because we love you."

That made me want to start crying again. I somehow kept the tears at bay this time, and in a halting voice, I told my dad everything. Well, not *everything* everything. There was no reason to tell him about losing my virginity to Jacob, but my dad was a smart guy and could put the pieces together. When I told him about sharing a hotel room with Jacob in Vancouver, my dad kept looking at the ceiling, as if it would provide divine intervention.

"So you were right," I finished, grabbing more tissues. "He didn't give a shit about me. He wanted to win that money and use any method to get it. The worst of it is, if I'd listened to you about the design I ended up submitting, I probably could have won. I was too stubborn to listen, and I let everyone down."

My voice broke, and I crumpled up the tissues in my hand.

"Oh, honey," my dad said, "you've never let me down."

"Of course I let you down. I was going to use that money to make the store even better, but I've done nothing but fuck things up."

"Now, that's a load of crap, and you know it." My dad sighed. "I know I've been hard on you, Dani, and I'm realizing just now that I've been *too* hard on you. You were always so strong, so capable, that sometimes it made me forget that you can be vulnerable, too. I'm sorry about that. Sorrier than I can say."

He took the crumpled-up tissues from my hand. "You've

done an amazing job running the store. I couldn't be prouder. And just because you didn't win this competition, it doesn't mean you can't win next year. You can accomplish whatever you set your mind to."

My heart lifted with each word he said. I hadn't realized how much I needed to hear what he was saying. Although Jacob had wounded me deeply, his betrayal couldn't break me, not with the support of my annoying, nosy, lovable family.

"I still think that boy shouldn't have won in the first place," said my dad caustically, "but I believe you when you say he didn't outright copy you."

"You were right about the Wests: I should've stayed away from Jacob."

"We've all gotten mixed up with people we shouldn't."

I raised an eyebrow. "Like who?"

My dad leaned back in his chair, his expression faraway. "Did I ever tell you about Camilla Langdon?" He let out a whistle. "I dated her before I met your mother. Everybody in town knew she was bad news, but I didn't listen."

"So what happened?"

"I proposed, she laughed at me, and then she ran off with one of the Sanders' boys." My dad's expression darkened. "That's why we never, ever buy compost from their store."

"Their compost is tainted? Who knew. I thought it was just shitty."

"It *is* shitty." My dad smiled wryly. "Do you want to return to dinner, or do you want to sneak out before your mom and sisters jump on you?"

I chose the latter, and I snuck out of the house with my dad's help and walked home. They could always come banging on my door, of course, but at least this gave me a little time to collect my thoughts before they started demanding answers.

I didn't have much time to be alone, though. When I heard the knock on my door, I thought it was my family. I even had the stupid thought that it could be Jacob. But it was Anna, who looked fit to be tied.

"Why haven't you been answering my messages?" she demanded, coming inside my apartment. "I thought you were dead."

"I replied to one message."

"Yeah, one. Out of at least six. So, what's the deal? I haven't seen you in forever." She looked at me more closely, probably noticing my still bloodshot eyes and red nose. "Okay, you look like shit. Spill, woman."

I did spill, except unlike with my dad, I told her the details regarding Jacob and me. I probably told her too much, but Anna had a way of weaseling information out of people that you realized later had been major TMI.

"And you haven't heard from him since?" she asked.

Kevin hopped onto my lap and I petted him absently. "Nope. Total radio silence."

"Well, clearly he's a fuck weasel. I'm glad you told him off. But..."

I scratched Kevin behind his ears, one of which had lost its tip before I'd adopted him. "But?"

"Maybe it's not as black and white as it seems."

I stared at her. "Seriously?"

"No, hear me out." She sat forward. "Why didn't he totally ghost on you the second he'd gotten what he wanted? That makes no sense. And what guy not only dresses up in a tux to make up for standing you up for prom, but makes sure your first time is legen-fucking-dary?"

"It wasn't that great," I lied.

"Bullshit. I saw you five days later and you were still having an orgasm."

"I don't think that's humanly possible."

"Look, I'm not saying you shouldn't be pissed or that he didn't fuck up. He did. He's a douche for this whole thing. But what if he's a douche who knows he screwed up and maybe, just maybe, he cares enough about you to make things right?"

I snorted. "If that were true, he would've contacted me by now."

"Would you have listened to him?"

I didn't answer, because we both knew what I would've told him. *Go fall off a cliff*, or some iteration of that.

"You don't have to act like he didn't hurt you, but if you love him, maybe hear him out. You don't have to forgive him. But he wasn't totally wrong about how you push people away."

I scowled. "Why are you on his side?"

"Bitch, I'm always on your side, which is why I'm here to tell you the truth." She smiled when Kevin climbed into her lap, the traitor. "You expect people to disappoint you. When you expect something, it'll happen. So then you're justified in keeping everyone at arm's length. Except me, of course. I wouldn't let you do that to me."

My head and heart hurt. I didn't know what I wanted to do anymore. Despite what he did, I missed Jacob terribly. Not just the sex, but that was a part of it. I missed that connection with him, the way he pushed me, the way he discovered not just my sexuality, but my squishy insides that were protected by a hard emotional exterior.

"I don't know if I can let myself trust him again," I whispered. "Because what if he lets me down again? How many times can I let a guy break my heart?"

"To be fair, you didn't really love him when you were a kid. You didn't know him. He was right about you putting him on a pedestal."

"I'm still not convinced you're really on my side."

"Oh, you're such a love bug," cooed Anna to Kevin, who was purring and drooling at the same time. "Purr, purr, purr."

"Concentrate," I said.

"Sorry. I don't know why you always say Kevin is a jerk. He loves me." She then said to me, "If Jacob tries to work things out, then hear him out. That's all I'm saying. Because I think if you don't, you'll regret it."

Later that evening, as I watched *Chopped* with Kevin now on my lap, I wondered if Jacob would even try to mend things with me. It had been three weeks already. Didn't that mean he'd moved on?

I hadn't moved on, though. I still loved him; I still wanted to be with him. Leaning down to kiss Kevin on his silky head, I murmured, "Why are men so stupid?", and Kevin, being a cat and a male, didn't feel like giving me an answer.

CHAPTER TWENTY-THREE

The following Monday, I went to the cafe two blocks from Buds and Blossoms to get my usual latte. I had about an hour before I needed to open the store, but I hadn't slept well and I thought I could get a jump-start on all the work I needed to get done.

"Dani? Is that you?"

I turned to see Tiffany McClain, now in line for coffee. She was dressed in scrubs, and she even looked tired, although she still managed to be beautiful despite the bags under her eyes.

"How's Kevin?" she asked.

Taking Kevin into the emergency vet felt like it had happened a million years ago, instead of just two months ago. "He's good. No more lily incidents."

"Oh, Dani, I'd love for you to meet my fiancée." A woman with dark brown skin and hair as dark as midnight approached. "Lola, this is Dani. We went to school together as kids."

I shook hands with Lola, wondering if their combined beauty would melt my eyeballs. It was like staring into the sun.

Lola, Tiffany, and I chatted for a few minutes until everyone received their coffee and needed to go on their separate ways. After Lola left for work—she worked as a loan officer at a bank—Tiffany followed me outside.

"So, this probably isn't my place to say anything," she said suddenly, "but since Jacob has come back, we've gotten to be friends again." She hurried on. "Just friends, though. Lola and I are very much in a committed relationship, and I don't date men anymore. Anyway, he told me about you…and him. And what happened in Los Angeles."

My face burned. Had Jacob seriously talked to his ex-girlfriend while completely ghosting on me? Now I was pissed.

"I'm not sure why you're telling me this," I ground out.

"I know. I'm doing a terrible job." She laughed awkwardly. "He only told me the bare bones. But the real reason I'm talking to you is because their store is in trouble."

"Why? Because Jacob took it over?"

"No, it was already deep in the red. It's to the point that his parents are about to lose everything: their house, their retirement. Everything." Tiffany tapped her red-painted fingernails against her coffee cup. "Lola told me. I realize giving you this information isn't exactly aboveboard, but I felt like you should know. If it made any difference to how you felt about Jacob."

Tiffany could have knocked me over with one flick of her nails, I was so stunned. Never in a million years would I have thought that Jacob's store was in trouble. He'd hinted at it, I realized. Why hadn't I asked more questions?

Then again, he'd wanted the prize money badly enough to betray me, the woman he said he loved.

"Look, I'll let you go, but I just know from experience that it's too easy to see the worst in people, not the best. But that's how you end up alone." Tiffany smiled sadly. "I'm lucky Lola and I got a second chance. That's all."

I didn't stop to think about my next actions. I texted Judith, told her that I needed her to open the store because an emergency came up, and was relieved when she said she'd be there within the hour.

Then I went looking for Jacob.

I went to his apartment complex (he'd since given me his exact address), and knocked on his door. No answer. I texted him; I called him in the meanwhile. Again, no answer.

I went straight to his parents' house. When Kenneth West answered the door, my voice disappeared because he looked so much like Jacob that it was physically painful to look at him. He was hunched over a bit, a cane in his right hand.

"Is Jacob here?" I said, my heart in my throat.

Kenneth narrowed his eyes at me. "You're one of the Wright girls," he said. The left side of his face drooped, and I almost didn't understand what he was saying.

"Yes, I'm Dani. It's nice to see you. I hope you liked the quiche. Is Jacob here?"

"Ken, who is it?" Jacob's mom, Heidi, came to the door. She was blonde like her son, but at least a half a head shorter than him. "Oh, hello. Are you here for your pie pan? I meant to stop by and return it to you. It was sweet of you to bring it by."

I wanted to scream. "You're welcome. Is Jacob here?"

Heidi's perfectly plucked eyebrows winged to her forehead. "Jacob? No, dear."

"Do you know where he is?"

Kenneth grunted. "You're the girl he's been pining after, aren't you? He never said who it was, but it makes sense. Why he was so riled up about doing the competition." He sighed. "He probably was right. You know you're old when your kid knows better than you."

"Oh, you know what," said Heidi, like her husband hadn't said anything, "Jacob should be at the greenhouse today. I'll give you the address."

After what felt like hours, Heidi returned with a handwritten address, smiled at me, and led her husband back inside. But not before Kenneth essentially confirmed what Tiffany had told me already, except not in so many words. I wondered if his stroke made him more prone to telling people details he wouldn't have given out when he'd been well.

THE GREENHOUSE WAS north of the city, an almost thirty-minute drive. By the time I arrived, my coffee was cold, my palms were sweaty, and I wasn't sure if I wanted to wring Jacob's neck or kiss him until we couldn't breathe.

The greenhouse was one of a dozen on the property, each one about twenty feet apart. The area seemed deserted; there were only two other cars in the parking lot.

I found him trimming hyacinths. The sweet smell of them wafted to me; he hadn't heard me come inside.

"Why didn't you tell me your shop was in trouble?" I said to the back of his head.

He stilled, his shoulders stiffening. I drank in the line of his back, the wave of his hair. It had grown since I'd last seen him, enough that it brushed his collar. But when he stood up and turned toward me and I saw his face, I almost collapsed—with relief, with love, with confusion.

"How did you find out?" was all he said.

"Your dad, for one." I decided not to mention Tiffany spilling the beans.

His mouth screwed up into a mockery of a smile. "I didn't know how badly the store was doing until it was too late to turn it around. Then my dad got sick, and the medical bills started piling up. Not only had my parents taken out a second mortgage on their house, but they used all of their savings to dig the store out. Suddenly they had to use their retirement to pay for the hospital stay.

"My dad isn't old enough for Medicare," Jacob added, "his insurance is shitty, and—well, you can guess the rest."

"I'm so sorry." I meant it.

"Don't be. I should've found a different way to get the money."

"It didn't sound like you had a choice."

Jacob shook his head. "The arrangement was actually mine, for the most part. I mean, it was *your* idea, but everything else was me. My dad had some input, but he can't do things like he used to. I knew I should stop, especially as things between us…progressed. I thought I could get away with winning and you never finding out, that it was the price I'd had to pay."

His eyes darkened. "But the price was too high. Because I never thought it would mean losing the woman I loved. Still love."

"Oh, Jacob." I sighed.

He reached inside a bag near his feet and drew out an envelope. "I was going to drop this off for you today."

I frowned, opening it. Had he written me a Dear John letter? Or the opposite of one? As I began to read it, I realized it had nothing to do with our relationship. Well, everything and nothing.

"You disqualified yourself?" I whispered.

"I explained what I did, and I told the judges I shouldn't have the prize. They agreed. Since you got second place, now you've won it. It's yours, Dani. It should've been yours to begin with. I know it can't make up for what I did, but it's a start."

I couldn't stop the tears this time. "This was never about the money. It was about the fact that you lied to me, and used me, and then told me you loved me. I trusted you with everything."

"I know." He cupped my face, staring into my eyes. "I know. I'm sorry. If you give me a second chance, I'll make it up to you every way I can. Starting with letting you have this money."

"I don't want the money!" I covered my face, sobbing. "How can you be so smart and such an idiot at the same time?"

He looked adorably confused now. "What?"

"I just wanted to know that you really loved me. Me, the weird plant girl. That's all I really wanted."

"Christ, Dani." He moved my hands away from my face. "I love you so much that I was going insane, waiting for the fucking convention to give me a damn answer about the prize money. It was like pulling teeth, except all the people were old and took twenty years to answer all of two emails."

I laughed. "I'm so sorry for your pain and anguish."

"Put me out of my misery, then. Tell me you still love me."

"Okay, now you really are stupid." I threw my arms around his neck and kissed him, because it was easier to show than to tell right then.

Jacob seemed to get what I meant pretty easily. He kissed me until I couldn't breathe, his mouth hard and slanted over mine, kissing me until my lips felt bruised.

"You love me?" he demanded. "Say it."

"I love you. Jacob West, I've loved you since I was five years old and you made me that dandelion crown. How can you not know that?"

He smiled, that kind of smile that's like having rays of sunshine penetrate your heart. Reaching down near the bag where he'd pulled out the letter, he went down on one knee and presented me with a dandelion crown.

"Because you told me you tore up the other one," he said simply. "And I'll make it my life's mission that you never have a reason to tear this one up. I was going to bring it by your place later, but since you're here…"

It was like the most ridiculous pseudo proposal ever that I started laughing, but it was through tears, and I couldn't say anything except, "You are the worst person *ever*."

I took the crown and placed it on my head. It was a bit lopsided, which made me love it even more.

"You look beautiful," he said, completely sincere.

"I'm wearing a crown made of weeds, but I believe you." I kissed him again, and soon the kiss heated up into something way more interesting than just a handsy make-out session.

Jacob pushed pots and tools off of the nearby table, the collection of items making a nice crashing sound. I would've chastised him for breaking perfectly good pottery, but then he was setting me on the table, never breaking the kiss, and suddenly I didn't give two solitary shits about broken pottery. Not with Jacob's hands and mouth on me.

It had been way too damn long.

"I can't go slow," he said, echoing my thoughts. "I need you way too badly."

"If it makes you feel better, I've been basically soaked since the second I saw the back of your head. I should've brought an extra pair of panties." I sighed in mock annoyance.

Jacob hummed under his breath as he cupped my breasts. "Sounds like a real problem. I'll help you with that."

"You're always so helpful—" The word was cut off when he sucked my nipple through my bra, and the friction of the lace against the swollen peak was almost painful. Painfully good.

I was very glad that I'd worn shorts and flip-flops today. What would happen in wintertime, with all the boots and pants and socks and coats? I realized I hadn't had sex yet in the winter, but I was very much looking forward to it, since Jacob would be the one stripping me down, layer by layer.

"Wait," I said suddenly. I looked around. "What if someone sees us?"

Jacob considered the question, before pulling my shirt down to cover my breasts. "No one can see the rest of you through all of the greenery." His smile turned wicked. "You'll have to be very quiet, though. Otherwise somebody might come to see what's wrong."

"You're assuming you can get me to make a lot of noise."

He cocked an eyebrow. "Did you just dare me?" He rolled my panties down my legs and spread my legs in a smooth movement. "That was a very bad idea, sweetheart, because now I'm going to have to make you suffer."

"Oh, noooooooo…"

Parting my pussy lips, he groaned when he saw how wet I was already. I had to bite my lip to keep from crying out when he licked me, slowly drawing more moisture from my body. I grabbed onto his hair, and he grunted when I pulled rather hard on the golden strands.

"This pussy is mine," he said, almost growling, the vibrations of his voice enhancing the sensations he was coaxing from me. "And I'm the only man who's ever seen it, tasted it, and fucked it. Do you know how hot that is, Dani? That your tight little pussy was saved just for me?"

"I didn't mean to save it." I squealed when he sucked on my clit. "It just never happened before."

Jacob's expression was wry. "Baby, we need to work on your dirty talk and foreplay. Let a man have his fantasy, all right?"

"I am glad it was you, though." I leaned my head back, my thighs burning as Jacob held them apart to keep me wide and open for him. "I'm so glad it was you. I think I was waiting for you, actually." I sighed and moaned at the same time as he pressed two fingers inside me as he thumbed my clit.

"Say it again, Dani." He rubbed harder.

"Which part?" I felt my orgasm drawing closer, and if I weren't so desperate for it, I would've been embarrassed by the wet sounds my pussy made with each thrust of Jacob's fingers inside me.

"The part where you waited for me."

I squealed when he found that magical spot inside me that set fireworks off in my brain. I couldn't think now. "It's always been you. I told you that. Oh my God, please, please—"

He mouthed my clit again, and that was all it took to make me come. I shook so hard the table rattled. Jacob lapped at my pussy as I came and came until I was boneless. I had to hang onto his shoulders, otherwise I would've slid onto the floor and never have gotten up again.

He didn't give me time to recover, though. Freeing his cock from his jeans, he thrust inside my still clenching channel until he was balls deep. I couldn't get enough air inside my lungs. As he pounded into me, our bodies slapping together, my release seemed to go on and on and coiled more tightly deep in my belly again. I was going to come so hard that I would probably die, and I didn't even care.

Jacob had hooked his arms under my legs, which gave him complete control of how fast and how deep he fucked me.

"Look at how you take my cock," he said. "So tight and so wet for me as I take this pussy and fill it."

I looked down at where we were joined, and a full-body shiver racked my body. Jacob wouldn't let me look away now. I watched him stuff me, over and over again, my pussy tightening around him until he could barely thrust back inside.

"I'm coming," I screamed. "I'm coming, I'm coming—"

Jacob laughed roughly and put a hand over my mouth. So much for keeping quiet. When he pushed one last time inside me, his pelvis glancing off of my clit, that was it. I died. I exploded, and as he poured his seed inside me until it leaked out of me onto the table, I was pretty sure every bone, every muscle, every internal organ just melted away.

He groaned loudly into my ear as his orgasm took over. I loved watching him shake, suddenly losing that control he was so good at. And the woman who'd done it was *me*. Yeah, I was a little proud of myself for that, I had to admit.

I whimpered when he finally pulled out of me. He drew a finger lightly through my folds, smearing his come around and looking inordinately proud of himself.

"I'm going to be dripping out of you for the rest of day," he whispered into my ear. "Which is probably the hottest thing ever."

I sighed. "You're such a man."

"But you love it."

"My burden in life, I guess."

After we'd cleaned up as best as you can do in a greenhouse, I realized I hadn't asked Jacob the most pressing question that had been on my mind. Until he'd kissed me and my mind had apparently gone utterly blank.

"What are you going to do about the store? Your parents?" I said. "What'll happen if you don't have that money?"

"We'll have to close, file for bankruptcy. I've talked to an attorney, and I hope we can save their house, but there's no guarantee."

How could I take this money when Jacob's parents would be out on the street, his dad still not completely well? Would they have to move in with Jacob, three people in a one-bedroom apartment?

"I have some money, so I can help my parents get a place, but it won't be in the city. It's too expensive now." Jacob sighed. "But it's tricky, because my dad needs to be close to his doctors, but I'm not sure what the solution is."

The idea came to me, so quickly that it immediately felt right. "I'll buy you out."

Jacob's forehead creased. "What?"

"I mean, it might be a terrible idea. But what if we combined our stores somehow? I wanted to expand Buds and Blossoms into teaching classes. We could use your location for that."

"Dani, I love you for the suggestion, but all you're going to get is debt and more debt."

"And I love you for thinking I'd let you deal with this without my help." I brushed Jacob's hair from his forehead. "Can't we at least try? The money from the competition alone should be a huge help."

Jacob considered my proposal, and the gray cloud that had come over his face seemed to lift. "I still don't want your money."

"Then think of it as *our* money."

"It'll probably be a total disaster, if we do this."

"Probably."

"Our parents will never forgive us."

"Also true."

He pressed his forehead against mine. "It's totally crazy."

"But that's what we're good at."

Jacob laughed, shaking his head, and proceeded to show me how crazy the two of us could really be together.

EPILOGUE

Jacob

W hen I moved back to Seattle six months ago, I never expected that I'd be moving into a condo with the girl who'd been my childhood friend years ago and who turned out to be my soulmate, or that her evil cat would decide that he actually loved me, or that we'd be in the process of merging our stores together, despite the many protests of our parents.

But life has a way of making the unexpected exactly what you needed. And somehow the universe had known I needed Dandelion Wright, and I'd somehow managed to get a second (or really, third) chance with her.

"Kevin, look at your new window!" Dani lifted her ridiculously mangy cat up to show him the view of Lake Union. "You'll be able to watch all the birds."

Kevin yawned, already bored. He wiggled to get down and proceeded to get into one of the many empty boxes to take a nap. I took the opportunity to watch Dani bend over one of the boxes she'd been unpacking, admiring the round curve of her ass through her skinny jeans.

The only reason I didn't bend her over the only chair that had been brought in so far and enjoy every inch of her curves was because we actually needed things in these boxes. Plus, the movers were still coming in and out with our stuff, so that put a bit of a damper on my libido. But considering I wanted Dani practically all the time, it was only a slight, temporary damper.

I wrapped my arms around her waist. "I'm looking forward to fucking you right in front of this window."

She let out a startled laugh. "I didn't think you were into having people watch us."

"I'm not. We'd do it at night and keep the lights off. Besides, we're up high enough that nobody could see us."

"I'm not sure I'd want to test that theory. Besides, we'd get the glass all smudged."

I bit the side of her neck, and she giggled.

Yeah, I was a goner for her. Had been the second I'd come into her store and seen her all flustered with that vase stuck on her hand. She'd looked so pretty, flushed and frustrated, her magnificent tits heaving. I'd had a hard-on within seconds and it had taken all of my self-control not to kiss her sassy mouth when she'd mouthed off at me.

"Oh, I heard from the bank," said Dani, turning inside the circle of my arms. "We have an appointment next week to discuss merging the businesses."

"And so you can take on all of our debt." I still didn't love the idea, but Dani could be just as persuasive—and stubborn —as me when she wanted.

"Think of it as a business deal. I'm buying you out for my own gain."

"It's a terrible deal, then."

She patted my cheek. "Not if it helps you and your parents. Who, I think, like me now."

"Which is to say your parents still don't like *me.*"

She winced. When we'd first announced our relationship to our respective families, it had been total chaos. Her parents had objected, my parents had objected, and everyone had acted like the world was going to end when we threw in the additional bombshell of merging the two businesses. The only two who'd been supportive had been Dani's sisters.

"I guess it's better than you both committing suicide," Kate had said practically. "You know, if we're ending this whole *Romeo and Juliet* thing."

Mari had told me in no uncertain terms that if I hurt Dani, she'd chop off my balls. Except she said it so sweetly that I hadn't been sure she'd been serious until I'd asked Dani about it.

"After the David thing? Yeah, she's serious. She'll kill you in your sleep." Dani had said it so cheerfully that I'd been a little afraid to fall asleep that night.

The Wright sisters were fucking terrifying when they had a mind to be.

"My parents will come around," said Dani as the movers returned with more of our stuff. "Once they realize this will be better for everyone, and that we're serious about each other."

I could see hurt flash across her face: her dad had suggested more than once that I was still messing with her for my own gain, which had resulted in our first ever argument as a couple when I'd wanted to confront her dad and she'd told me to stay out of it.

I had confronted her dad later on, although Dani had no idea. I'd sworn her dad to keep his mouth shut, and he'd actually agreed. The ring in my pocket felt heavy as I waited for the movers to finish up. I'd planned to propose after we'd settled in and weren't living out of suitcases, but I couldn't wait. I wanted to show the world that I was completely serious about Dani and me—beyond the whole "I love her" and moving in together thing. Apparently neither of those counted.

The movers finished just as it started to rain, the drops pattering against the window. Fall was beginning to settle on the city, the leaves dipped in shades of gold and umber and crimson. I'd forgotten how beautiful it was here. New York had its merits, but there was something about the Pacific Northwest that always called you back.

Night had fallen when Dani and I stood at the window. The view was absolutely spectacular: the city skyline in the distance, the dark shadow of Lake Union below us. I could make out a sliver of the moon in the eastern part of the sky.

"Are you happy?" I said.

Dani rested her hands on my arms that I'd wrapped around her. "Perfectly, stupidly, disgustingly happy."

"Do you think you could be even happier?"

She tilted her head back to look at me. "Maybe? I'm a little worried now."

When I went down on one knee, she gave me a confused look. Then understanding filled her expression when I pulled out the ring.

"Dandelion, I want to make you the happiest woman on

earth," I said. I opened the ring box, showing her the golden topaz ring inside, the same color as her namesake. "I know it's fast and I know we hadn't really talked about this, but—"

"Yes," she burst out. "Yes, yes, yes, I'll be your wife so hard you won't know what hit you."

She threw herself into my arms, which completely overset my balance, since I was on one knee. We tumbled to the floor and knocked over a vase Dani had just unpacked. Luckily, it didn't break, but the sound startled Kevin, who was still napping in his box. He jumped almost as high as the ceiling and then sprinted to the bedroom to hide under the bed for the foreseeable future.

"Well, that was a disaster," I said. I took the ring from the box and placed it on Dani's ring finger before placing the vase back onto the table.

"But we've always been a disaster." She kissed me, which just gave me a great reason to roll her under me until she was moaning my name. It usually took ten seconds, tops, to get her there.

This time it only took four.

We were lying on the rug, catching our breaths, when Dani's phone rang. She reached for it from the coffee table, reading the text message on the screen. Her expression went from sated to utterly confused in a blink.

"What is it?" I tried to take her phone from her.

"It's Mari. She's in Vegas right now." Dani showed me the message. It took me a second to understand what I'd just read.

I got married last night. His name is Liam. That's all I know.

And in a second message:

Don't tell Mom and Dad. They'll kill me.

Into the cloying silence that had settled over us, I said, "Well, so much for us being the biggest disasters in the family."

ABOUT THE AUTHOR

A coffee addict and cat lover, Iris Morland writes sexy and funny contemporary romances. If she's not reading or writing, she enjoys binging on Netflix shows and cooking something delicious.